**DO NOT REMOVE
CARDS FROM POCKET**

ALLEN COUNTY PUBLIC LIBRARY

FORT WAYNE, INDIANA 46802

You may return this book to any agency, branch,
or bookmobile of the Allen County Public Library.

DEMCO

Where Do You Put the Horse?

ESSAYS BY

Paul Metcalf

The Dalkey Archive Press, 1986

Some of the essays in this book have previously appeared in the following publications: *A Hundred Posters, Aperture, Athanor, Glitch, Granite, Hawk Wind, Kulchur, Margins, Mulch, Northern Lights, Paper Air, Parnassus, Primer, Prose, Red Hand Book, San Francisco Review of Books, Sarcophagus, Stump, Tansy, The Berkshire Eagle, The Mickle Street Review, The Review of Contemporary Fiction, The Third Berkshire Anthology, Truck, United Artists, Valley Advocate, Vort,* and #. The preface to *Time in New England* appeared in *Time in New England*, Photographs by Paul Strand. Aperture, Inc., Millerton, New York, 1980.

Partially funded by grants from The National Endowments for the Arts and The Illinois Arts Council.

Cover photo by Marilyn Patti

The Dalkey Archive Press
1817 79th Avenue
Elmwood Park, IL 60635 USA

Where Do You Put the Horse?

Essays By

Paul Metcalf

Contents

1

The Categories

It is strange that, at all visible levels, American literature is so neatly organized into exclusive territories, Poetry and Fiction. Poets and Writers, Inc., has published two separate directories: American Fiction Writers and American Poets. Most universities hire a poet-in-residence and a fiction-writer-in-residence. Editors accept one or the other, poetry or fiction, and there is never a question as to which is which.

In practice, there are two warring tyrannies at work here: fiction writers make money . . . poets have class, or status, or altitude. As a fiction writer, I have a trade, a profession, I sell my wares, just about as fast as I can manufacture them . . . as a poet, I may have a job (poet-in-residence), but I'm above the marketplace, my gems are beyond price, and I look more than a little down on you.

All of this is more than a little ridiculous . . . particularly in view of the subliminal drive in two of our major forebears—Poe and Melville—to violate the questionable boundary between the two genres.

Poe and Melville wrote both poetry and prose. Poe's poetry was rhythmical and glittering, and, to the modern ear, too musical-mechanical to command respect. Melville wrote heavy-handed, laboring poetry. But both Poe and Melville wrote a prose that reached passionately toward the borders, prose full of feeling (both inward and outward), full of music, with the "higher sense," whatever you want to call it . . . Poe's and Melville's prose, almost without exception, is prose-poetry.

There are other examples, I'm sure, in our nineteenth-century heritage. Doesn't *The Red Badge of Courage* have that kind of passion? And Whitman, God knows, had to invent a poetry, a verse of his own—the raw goods of which were linsey-woolsey.

Perhaps this is what I'm after: that the reach in our literature, our tradition (and we have an example of this in as recent a writer as Carl Sauer), originates in prose, a dirt-prose, that in the power and energy

5

of its own passion forces the gates of poetry. No wooden horse, no gimmicks—just sheer force.

In the face of this tradition—which, to me, has the force of an avalanche—it seems strange to see our official, functional world falling back into the little inherited European boxes that so antedate what is happening today and what has been happening for so many years.

1977

2

Blast-Off

The first encounter in *Tropic of Cancer* involves Miller and a girl in an impatience of passion: they try it sitting down, they try it standing up, and the heat is too intense—he infuriates her by coming all over her dress while dancing, and this is the tipoff: the Whitman, the exhibitionist, the spraying of semen over exteriors, for the glitter of it—semen in place of ink, as the liquid of literature.

Everything, latterly, about the placing of European seed in virginal American soil has been external, exploited, public, the shoot-'em-ups are ever with us, we love nothing so much as exposé. Because they couldn't get *into* it, they had to get *out* to it: the West. (Latterly, that is, as opposed to the early West, the forested Appalachians that Jefferson contemplated at Monticello—this was a land to be penetrated privately, as Boone penetrated it.)

This is the problem, what Pound recognized as our failure to distinguish between the public and the private: the most private act being the placing of seed exactly, goddammit, where it belongs.

Now . . . with the conquest of the West, the *Cowboy*—the hero of the shoot-'em-ups—has been replaced by the *Astronaut*, who embodies for the American male the old dream of perpetual ejaculation, a fountain, one's own, a fountainhead, Old Faithful . . .

> (peripheral,
> off target,
> dispersed & exposed,
> [solo,
> hetero, homo])

shooting up into space!

1973

3

Robert Creeley

The Island. By Robert Creeley

Creeley has a peculiar affinity for the word *divers*—it is the name he gave to the press he operated in Mallorca, and he uses it frequently in *The Island*, usually in the sense of *various*, but always, within it (everything is at least double), the marine sense, the diver not as Olson, the wild plunge, as Olson got it from Melville ("I love all men who dive," or some such) but quietly, piercing the fathoms as if they were nothing, to a known goal. And here the image becomes the needle with which the Joan of the book (with John characteristically, helplessly absent) pierced and aborted their would-be child. Quiet. And fierce. And there is the later, greater image, John fishing his unflushable son out of the toilet bowl, carrying him in newspaper to the ash can.

Others go about it differently, Pynchon and Sigal come to mind, riding the storm. . . . Creeley, and perhaps Douglas Woolf, have these corners they get into, the very opposite of "retreats"— Mallorca, Guatemala, the desert, whathaveyou, from which they get full engagement, full purchase.

The Needle. And, here is your son. He won't flush. Get rid of him. Life, the Life in him, has gotten too big.

The book buds out in sunshine, full of happiness and relaxation (they say that Hank Aaron, when he comes to bat, falls asleep between pitches) . . . there is felicitous assumption of mantles, the ease with which he does this is childlike and lovely: Lawrence, Williams, Anderson . . . but don't let it fool you—it is Creeley all the time. And just Creeley. And the boat isn't rocking.

The *New York Times* got some ox-head to review it, who worried at length about the syntax . . . missed it altogether. Read it. Read it quietly, so you won't wake him.

1964

8

4

Clancy Sigal

Going Away. By Clancy Sigal

Sportswriters have a phrase they like to use, in speaking of a top-notch pro quarterback: he picks the defense to pieces. Well, a game, like a book or a play, is a frame in which to measure endeavor. I'm not quite sure what Clancy Sigal set out to do in *Going Away*, probably just keeping up with the thing was all he could manage. But he has triumphed over a tragedy that defeats so many of us, re-encountering as writers what our forepappies faced: The Opposition, The Defense: The Land.

The easy part of it, historically, was over early, the East-Coastal Indians were disorganized, the land tenable, the marine-commercial cities became quickly European. And west of this, Appalachia, with its rolling hills and old, forested mountains, had a sense about it that the mind could cope with. Civilized. But west again was something else: the vastness, the flatness, the sameness (all the terms are clichés) and here the imagination staggered and halted. And part of it died. Men went on, the automatons that Lawrence speaks of in his preface to *Bottom Dogs*, but sensibility dropped behind, like the ludicrous paraphernalia dropped out of the covered wagons, bit by bit, all the wrong things brought.

This, then, was and is The Opposition. And as we awaken to the totality of it, we are unable to free ourselves of just that, the totality, and we are, just as it is, flattened.

Sigal begins his book at The End: Hollywood, and works back east, counter to historical flow—just as, in *Moby-Dick*, Melville violated the same dynamic, as well as personal experience, and sailed his ship west-to-east. The comparison is valid. And, once begun, Sigal picks the defense to pieces and doesn't stop until he's headed down the Narrows, for Europe, a thousand or so pages away. And he's done it. The full game. Of course, he's a little nutty at the time, but how else do you do it?

9

The point is, that Awful Totality, he doesn't let that defeat him at the start (or, the other side of the coin, make a jingo out of it)—it's all there, but he picks it to pieces, one by one, the steps are taken with care and deliberation, and, in the end, we've had it. All of it. No other book that I know accomplishes this.

1962

5

Play It Again, Sam

Following is a reconstruction of a conversation I held 7 May 1976 with my daughter Adrienne—

Adrienne— I think I know what your problem is. You know, everybody has a problem.
Paul— Oh?
Adrienne— You're a frustrated musician. I think if you'd been brought up in a musical household you'd have become a musician or composer, but because it was a literary household you turned to writing.
Paul— You've been reading some of my books?
Adrienne— Yes. *Apalache.*
Paul— That's funny. Because as a child I was forced to take piano lessons. I hated it, wouldn't practice. They tried me on a clarinet and that didn't take either.

*

Paul— Perhaps you can say I've brought music to literature.
Adrienne— Uh-uh. You've got it backwards. You've brought literature to music.

*

Adrienne— You know, I really can't handle it. When I think that you're my father—and you wrote this book—and you're this guy I know—and I'm so moved by the book—all this, all together, I can't handle it, it's more than I can take.

*

Adrienne— I think the reason some people have difficulty reading

11

your writing, they're looking for a beginning and an end, and there isn't any. It's like listening to a piece of music, it's what's happening right now. . . . I'm not musically inclined, but music has been a part of some of the most important things in my life.

N.d.

6

The Poet and History

The following was prepared as a lecture for a class at the University of Massachusetts.

The late poet Charles Olson could at times become absolutely obsessed with some given period of history. It has been said of him that he could read Herodotus like a daily newspaper.

I can understand this because I have had similar experiences myself when I have become immersed—I think of it as just short of drowning—in, say, the pre-Columbian Indians of Peru, the early Michigan days of Henry Ford, the life of Christopher Columbus or of Herman Melville. Some time ago I wrote a documentary history of the Potomac River watershed, everything, from the Indians—John Smith—Lords Delaware, Calvert and Fairfax—the early adventurers, explorers and surveyors—George Washington and the Federal City—John Brown, the Civil War, John Wilkes Booth—the flora and fauna—on up to the latest disastrous report from the Environmental Protection Agency. I was, for a year of my life, swimming in the Potomac. The book is just now being prepared for publication, and as I go back to it, to any given point in it, touching again the results of my research, when I was soaked in it, and combining this with my sense of the area from various visits I have made there, I can enter an ethos, a precise local quality, that may include the people, the past, the landscape, the geography, the geology, the climate, the natural ecology, the innumerable human and man-made changes, with the dynamics of each—so that I see it, feel it, think it, sense it, today, as a totality of *was/is*. And I think the success of the writing, insofar as there is success, is the result of this permeation.

Perhaps because of my own ancestry and upbringing, I was set up for these attitudes and methods. As a great-grandson of Herman Melville and the son of his literary executrix, I was exposed early to an atmosphere of both literature and history, the past. For many years, as a youngster, I rebelled against all this, refused to have

13

anything to do with it. The Boston Red Sox certainly had a greater place in history than *Moby-Dick*. I think this was all very healthy. It was only later that I discovered that rebellion is a form of love.

The uses of history are not without danger. It's an easy trap. We're all familiar with the stodgy professor-type who retreated thirty years ago into, let's say, the eighteenth century and hasn't been heard from since. The retreat was okay, but the dynamics, the will, the energy, perhaps simply the imagination, were lacking to bring it all back to the here and now.

Of course the present may also become a trap: the man or woman, the newspaper reader, victimized by the topical; the person for whom language becomes a blunt instrument, who responds like Pavlov's dogs to the emotional and visceral, so that meretricious appetite and irritation spring from him when he is beaten with words like *communist, ecology, energy, Watergate.*

I would think of history—and the varieties of language that ride with it—as a vast resource into which one plunges with energy, comparable to sexual energy, demanding and focusing all one's vitalities. Following this, there is the second phase, which I learned absolutely from Charles Olson: History is important only insofar as it impinges on the present. First, the plunge, the descent into hell, the near-drowning, if you wish; then the return to the surface. Because, if you drown, who cares? And if you don't plunge, who cares?

For many of you, as students, it is a matter of conscience to study history. You are not "educated" unless you know history. But the words *conscience* and *consciousness* are close in sound, and in my sense of history,· particularly as matter for the poets, the barrier between these words is shattered and they become one.

The plunge, and the return. This uniting of history and the present makes the historian himself, as a physical being living in the present, an integral element of the material he is handling. What material is pertinent (or, in that ugly word, "relevant")? The answer: *anything*—anything with which the poet-historian, by the dynamics of his presence, by the intensity and authenticity of his researches, by the passion of his caring, can so engross us in his periods of history as to make them at least twenty times more powerful than today's newspaper—by making them more *present.*

Einstein tells us that time is circular—and Marshall McLuhan explicates what we already know, that, thanks to the marvels of electronics, all information, past and present, is now instantly and ubiquitously available. All this would seem to make history illusory or superfluous—if time is circular, then old-fashioned linear time, historical time, evolutionary time cannot be important. This is a great temptation, and today there is a vast world—I find it a weird world—inhabited by scientologists and science fictioneers, UFO seekers and Brooklyn Buddhists, evangelical Christians and home-study astrologers—an odd lot, to be sure—God knows what Einstein would make of them—but all of them, in this uncertain and corrupt world, escaping into constructs that avoid the hard and/or glorious realities of their own genetic and cultural heritage. History and evolution may appear to disappear—and it may be comforting to believe in the imminent end of the world. But the world, manifestly, does not end. And all that you are, past and present, once more comes into focus, every morning, when you awaken.

So you awaken. You've left college, gone into the world, taken a job, and you come home at the end of the day, tired. On the coffee table are *Playboy*, *Time*, *The Enquirer* and *The Springfield Republican*. On TV, Walter Cronkite, and Sonny and Cher. In the bookshelves—those impressive floor-to-ceiling mausoleums (above-ground burial)—are Literature and History. What do you pick up?

Some years ago the poet Jonathan Williams was given a short-term teaching assignment at the University of Illinois. He had a free hand to do as he pleased, so in preparation he began to think about downstate Illinois, rural Illinois: what is it that characterized the area? And the answer, obvious and everywhere, was *corn*. Illinois is the damnedest corn-growing area anywhere in the world. So he generated this enterprise on corn, involving students from any number of disciplines: poets, historians, plant biologists, agronomists, anthropologists, ethnologists, dancers, artists. A whole segment of the university just went sort of corn-crazy for a while. They found out about themselves, their place, their history, their inherited and current culture, their *was/is*. I imagine he must have given them—and they themselves—a terrific experience.

It's all there—all these endless and fascinating determinants in your lives.

It's just a question of what *you* do with them.

1975

15

7

Butting Heads with the Transcendentalists

I have difficulty dealing with philosophy because I view it as conclusions, or distillations, derived from experience—and, for purposes of philosophy, I am too directly involved with experience itself.

Whenever I find myself reaching a conclusion, or a meaning, or a philosophic concept, I instinctively plunge it back into the day-by-day, rebury it.

Answer a question not with an answer, nor with a question, but with an unthinking, demanding physical activity.

That too is a philosophy—*mens sana in corpore sano*—but I don't view it as such: I view it as the Head blotted out, at least for a time, in the sweat of the Body (and that, too, is a false dichotomy, Head and Body: the two are one).

The head ignites, produces its illuminations, and then reburies, not just questioning itself, but incarcerating, risking itself, totally.

This is one of the dangers of the Age of Literacy in which we live: the Head can escape, live a life of its own (the Age of Literate Affluence or Affluent Literacy)—the Head in orbit, circuiting the Earth of the Body.

Hitherto, this has been a luxury of the aristocracy: the priesthood of primitive cultures, and the first true philosophers of ancient Greece—a slave-supported society.

Now, everyone has a Philosophy of Life, and if he doesn't, he can go out and get one.

But I find myself thrown back, or throwing myself back, into pre-thought, into plain experience. Which is why I dismiss Emerson—and am suspicious of Thoreau (I don't believe in transcending *anything*)—the Head will always rise, the world is full of Heads—what's difficult is the Body: Whitman's persistent lists, Melville's cetological details . . . it's difficult to hold onto that, to persist in that, when the Head wants to talk—as, God knows, it always does.

If ours is an agnostic age, it is because God has grown tired of listening. He's wearing a set of those ear protectors worn in noisy factories. He lives in a factory of philosophers.

1977

8

Henry David! Henry David!
Where Are You, Henry David?

Stanley Cavell writes in *The Senses of Walden*:

> Here is another underlying perception, or paradox, of *Walden* as a whole—that what is most intimate is what is furthest away . . .

. . . .

> The writer has secrets to tell which can only be told to strangers.

. . . .

> The more deeply he [Thoreau] searches for independence from the Puritans, the more deeply, in every step and every word, he identifies with them—not only in their wild hopes, but in their wild denunciations of their betrayals of those hopes, in what has come to be called their jeremiads. (This is a standing difficulty for America's critics, as for Christianity's; Americans and Christians are prepared to say worse things about their own behavior than an outsider can readily imagine.)

. . . .

> America's best writers have offered one another the shock of recognition but not the faith of friendship, not daily belief. Perhaps this is why, or it is because, their voices seem to destroy one another. So they destroy one another for us. How is a tradition to come out of that?

Thoreau, in making himself a Neighbor, first makes himself a Stranger. A Neighbor is always a Stranger, this is essential—should a Neighbor become a Friend, then he is no longer either Stranger or Neighbor, he is Friend, and has dropped out of or risen above the formula. Thoreau was always and to the end a Neighbor, a Stranger.

"I have traveled a good deal in Concord" . . . as Melville traveled the South Seas, anticipating the modern world, where the South Seas are a neighborhood.

As Thoreau was Neighbor and Stranger to Concord, so he was Neighbor and Stranger to Thoreau: that narrow but inviolate distance between the man and Concord, between the man and Thoreau. He could only get at himself through the year at Walden,

the bridge ... the book is a record of that attempt.
It is the nature of bridges to celebrate traffic—and separation.

1979

9

Incorporation: The Next Frontier

I have heard of some recent medical researches into the aging process. Among other subjects studied was the behavior of cancerous cells, and according to these researches, once a human cell becomes cancerous, it ceases to age.

This suggests wonderful possibilities to the imagination. It has always seemed to me that the philosophical approach to cancer—as a pathology, something evil, to be cut out, burned out, smashed, was questionable. This kind of thinking, behind most medical approaches to cancer, is suspiciously in harmony with the traditional American approach to Nature, the Landscape, Woodlands, etc.: if it's in the way, cut it down, burn it, get rid of it. Cut the trees, shoot the wildlife, level the land.

It has seemed to me for some time that no disease can be studied or treated in an abstract way, divorced from the culture in which it flourishes. I have been interested in the history of human illness— what illness or kind of illness seemed to dominate a given period of history. I imagine it's a difficult subject to research because of the constant changes in terminology—what would "an apoplectic fit" or "an attack of the ague" be called in modern medical terms? But instinct tells me that a given society, with given assumptions, given dominant drives, will harbor a given group of pathologies that seem to flourish in that particular culture. I don't know the history of the various types of cancer or of some of the other "modern" degenerative diseases (multiple sclerosis, muscular dystrophy, etc.), but it seems to me that these are diseases doing exceptionally well in this society at this time.

Certainly one of the dominant historical facts of the past hundred years—a prime determinant of American energies and an event with worldwide repercussions—is the closing of the frontier, the end of the limitless West. The precipitancy with which the white man proliferated across the landscape of this continent, the recognition of this precipitancy, will, even now today, take your breath away. The millions upon endless millions of bison roaming the prairie were reduced to a handful—largely in a period of only twenty years. And the door of the frontier slammed shut, just when the tide was in full flood.

One cannot resist the temptation to think of cancer as the playing out of those same energies—the drive to explore and dominate the landscape turned inward, exploring and dominating the host.

We Americans love to think of ourselves as a young country—and in many ways we surely are. It is only in recent years that the Sears Tower in Chicago has exceeded the Empire State Building in New York as the world's tallest building. How much longer can that sort of thing go on?

In cancerous cells, if recent researchers are correct, the aging process ceases. Imagine—cancer as the fountain of youth!

All this, at the very least, suggests a different philosophical approach. Destroy the landscape, and we destroy ourselves. So, instead of treating cancer as an evil, a pathology, to be eliminated, it becomes instead an energy, a source of hope, perhaps the ultimate vitality. The direction, then, is not toward eradication but toward diversion, harnessing—in the literal sense of the word, incorporation.

There are other areas, even more modern, in which some of these speculations break down. We read that a few teaspoonfuls of radioactive plutonium deposited in the water supply of a major city will produce malignancies by the millions. Facts like this are, to my imagination, simply unmanageable. We have to treat them as facts— we have no choice. But when the whole subject attains an inhuman, purely chemical level, such as this, my tendency is to return to the historical, cultural levels which may assume certain shapes in the imagination. This may be a cop-out—may very well be. But there is enough in these speculations that I have outlined to intrigue me. If I were a doctor, particularly a cancer researcher, I would want to think about them.

N.d.

21

10

Charles Olson

Charles Olson: A Gesture Towards Reconstitution

Several writers on whales—particularly modern writers, whose attitude is scientific and sympathetic, lacking the practical hostility of the earlier whalemen—speak of the shock on first coming in close contact with one of the great giants of the ocean. It is the onslaught of the sheer *size* of the creature, the very quality for which they had imaginatively prepared themselves and for which all preparation proves useless. The fact of finding oneself that close to such enormity simply intrudes, and all constructions planned for the experience melt and vanish.

It is in this sense that I remember swimming with Charles Olson at Edisto Beach, South Carolina. It was a warm day in late spring or early summer, the sun was bright, the air and ocean gentle. We swam out past the soft breakers, and, still standing on the shelf of sand or floating up and down with the waves, we let the ocean deal with us, while I needled him good-humoredly about Gertrude Stein, whose work he never liked.

Charles stood six-foot-eight or nine and weighed close to three hundred. He was in every part—head, features, shoulders, arms, all ways—an enormous man. Bobbing slowly with the waves, in a world so absolutely benign, with only his head, and occasionally his hirsute shoulders or the backs of his great hands, emerging above the glistening water surface—dipping his mouth now and then to take in and squirt out a mouthful of ocean—he gave me, swimming and floating close to him, that overwhelming sense of submarine enormity. And it is perhaps because I am not a small man myself—six-two and two-hundred pounds—tending in the same direction but stopped short of those geographies of physiology that he attained, that I found the experience so compelling.

When the world deals kindly with us, when Nature smiles in all her beneficence, we tend at times to think that this may not be permanent, and we may hinder our enjoyment of the occasion with

22

such thoughts. The placid whale may nuzzle peaceably to your side—and with a flip of its flukes destroy you. So with Charles: within our pleasant literary banter there was an edge not altogether benign—and this was related to my sense of the ocean-hidden vastness of the man.

His attitude toward his own size was filled with contradictions and extremes. He was prey, particularly in his younger years, to levels of embarrassment stemming from a concept of himself as at least a social alien and at worst some sort of monster. (He mentioned once, in his maturity, the difficulty he had in making it with the young chicks: "When I was younger, I was too tall; now I'm too old.") Yet he never let these feelings overwhelm or dominate him for long, he never succumbed to self-pity. He would instead come charging forth, in voice, intelligence and physical presence, and quite simply take over the world in which he found himself.

He had a habit, when we were sitting around talking, of rising from his chair, coming over to mine, pressing his thigh against the arm of my chair, forcing my eyes to rise to his, in that great head that occluded all other realities, and, his voice now deceptively gentle, allowing his bulk to carry the weight of his argument.

I have a cousin, Barton Chapin—a tall man himself, perhaps six-four—who was headmaster of a school in Buffalo at the time Charles was there teaching at the university, and I asked him once if they had ever met. He smiled, and recalled that he had been introduced to Charles at a party, when both were standing in a narrow doorway—and he had found dialogue there impossible.

On the same visit to Edisto Island, Charles spent the night with us in a little cottage we were borrowing, and all we could offer him for a bed was a narrow camp cot. The next morning, Charles, who normally slept until noon and often until twilight, was up and about early—incapable of dealing with that damned cot.

He came to visit us once in North Carolina, when our oldest daughter, Anne, was perhaps two or three, and he insisted on riding on the seesaw with her, laughing the fool all the time—and squatting to play in the sandbox with her.

In his relations with women, he seemed to go out of his way to dramatize his size. His two enduring connections were both with slight girls, shorter than average. The first, Connie, was perhaps four-foot-ten, and when they came for dinner in our first apartment—a tiny, low-ceilinged affair on West 18th Street—they sat side by side

23

on the double bed that served as a studio couch during the day. Connie, head and shoulders against the wall, spread her figure out straight, and her feet didn't reach the edge of the bed; Charles, his head and shoulders beside hers, spread torso and rump across the coverlet, while his thighs rose to mountainous knees, and calves descended to feet planted flat on the floor, seemingly in the middle of the room.

In contemporary professional basketball and football, where teams employ creatures of the same bulk and grace as Charles, such figures have perhaps become more commonplace. Forty years ago, however—which is about when I first met Charles—these people didn't seem to exist. (It is as though the genetic reservoir had quickly produced physiques for which there was a pressing cultural demand.) Charles, being physically unique, at least in his own day, reinforced a sense one had of him as an original.

When I first met him, I was perhaps fourteen, and he would have been twenty. I was living at home with my mother and father in Cambridge. My older brother was away at school, and I was shortly to leave. Charles had sought us out because of his interest in Melville—my mother was Melville's literary executrix, and this was the period of the Melville revival—all the scholars were zeroing in on us. Charles's health, which was never secure—partly because he abused it—was particularly bad at that time: he was going through the business of losing his teeth, and he suffered massive, accompanying head colds. With my brother and me gone or leaving, a residue of maternal instinct in my mother must have been called forth by this great colorful invalid. What a child to nurse! Take him in and nurse him she did.

Out of this emerged another strong element in him, the opposite and complement to the role of social alien, quasi-monster and absolute loner: *the need to belong.* So consumed was he at this time with Melville, so identified with him, that he determined to become one of us, to become a brother or cousin to me. I recall running down the list of my first cousins with him, reviewing who they were, where they were, what they were like, etc. My mother was his mother, and he had joined the bloodline. He had absolutely become a neo-Melville. The title of his book became *Call Me Ishmael.*

He wanted very much to meet my grandmother, Melville's youngest daughter, who was still living then. A sweet, gentle woman, she still so loathed her father that she refused to speak of him, to anyone. Mother knew full well that a meeting could never be managed—so one day she hid Charles in the bushes outside her mother's Boston apartment building, and, squatting as best he could behind the greenery, he caught a glimpse of this pathetic old lady as she emerged and made her way down the walk. That was enough, he was satisfied. He had identified with his grandmother.

This same drive—the need to belong—surfaced in other ways. Some years later, when he had made up his mind that the Melville blood-game wouldn't work, or he no longer wished it to, he discovered that the poet Yeats had great respect for the Hines family in Ireland. Charles's mother was a Hines, and this meant much to him, this genetic affirmation, coming as it did from Yeats.

Again, still later, when he was well into the *Maximus Poems*, and identifying with Gloucester and its fishing heritage, endeavoring to establish a brotherhood with those he considered his fellow fishermen, I visited him one day, at 28 Fort Square, and together we walked down to the fishing docks. It was a windy day and the boats were in harbor, the men on the docks mending nets. They indeed knew him, and talked with him for a while, civilly, about fish and weather—Charles, I felt, quietly staging all this for my benefit. But the fishermen were never warm, and after a while became quietly hostile: they stopped speaking English and spoke among themselves in Italian. Charles was slighted, and we moved off.

Counter to this, and much more powerful in his nature, was the role of dynamic outsider, radical independent—with time sense, money sense, practical sense—all the usual channels and weapons of interpersonal relations—absolutely fragmented.

Years ago, when he was still a young man, he secured a Guggenheim Fellowship, and all or a large part of the stipend came to him in a single check. He promptly went out and bought a horse for his mistress, and later commented, "They should have known better than to give it to me all at once."

Later, when he was living in Washington to be near Ezra Pound, I visited him, wiring ahead that I was coming. He failed to get my wire, so when I arrived at midday, I woke him up. Irritated and cordial at the same time, he tried to cook bacon and eggs for us, burning everything, laughing about it.

When he was at Black Mountain College, I found him one day, with Duncan and others, with matches and kerosene in a field of weeds, trying to burn the weeds off. They dumped kerosene, lit matches, ignited weeds, laughed, and nothing happened, nothing burned, all afternoon, an exercise in absolute futility and good humor.

While still at Black Mountain, he went to the West Coast for a short time, he, Betty and Charles Peter, taking the Pullman from Asheville. I offered to take care of his car for him while he was gone, running it occasionally to keep the battery up. We agreed to meet at the station. I arrived ahead of time and waited. The time arrived, the train pulled in, and I waited. The train pulled out, and I waited. Some ten or fifteen minutes later, in roars Charles—Chevrolet and Olson breathless. I think he was a little miffed with me for not having held the train, but I told him to his face that I didn't think he was reliable enough to warrant my intercession with the Southern Railway System. Slight irritation, but he got over it. Consulting with the stationmaster, we decided we had a good chance of beating the train to Knoxville, across the Great Smokies. With Charles at the wheel, Betty and the babe at his side, and me in the back, we passed a pint of booze back and forth, and fishtailed around the S-curves at insane speed. In Knoxville, the train was waiting for them in the station. I saw them boarded, and drove back alone, arriving home near dawn.

After Black Mountain had closed, and he was back in Gloucester, my wife Nancy and I, and Nicholas Dean, the photographer, drove out one day to see him. We arrived about midday, having announced our plans in advance. There was a note on the door, please do not disturb, he was sleeping. More than a little irritated, we went out for beer and lunch, becoming angrier as the beers went down. By three o'clock, we were ready for no further nonsense, so we went back. The note was still on the door, and no answer to our knocks. We yelled, kicked, beat the door, virtually dismantled it. No response. Nancy wanted to throw stones at the windows. Later, I heard, indirectly, that he was awake, and had heard us, but didn't come out because he was afraid to face Nancy.

Clark Coolidge told me a story of Charles walking in the street one night in Asheville when some redneck, probably drunk, approached Charles and hit him. Charles, according to the story, seemed to go through a deliberate process: he stopped, thought to himself, let's see now, I've been hit; yes; let's see now, where did it come from? over there? oh; yes; and—he flattened the guy.

(But that was a process of the mind moving through and generating

26

the processes of that great slow body. Where the mind moved alone, it moved instantly: "oxy-acetylene, we come in that close when we do come in.")

And Nick Dean tells a story of the great fisherman and mariner, Charles Olson, stepping into a canoe—and sinking it.

*

It was at Black Mountain College that Charles really came into his own. He arrived first on a commuting basis, maintaining his home in Washington, but it wasn't long before he moved in permanently—and when he did so, it quickly became apparent that he intended to take over. The college at that time was dominated by Josef Albers and the Bauhaus refugees, which gave it a distinct Germanic flavor, as well as a certain reputation and security, at least as much as an experimental college could hope to have. I don't know much of the details of this period, but Olson gradually moved in, the Germans moved out, and the great contemporary American period of the college came into being, attracting such figures as Creeley, Duncan, Dorn and Williams in writing, Kline and Motherwell in painting, Cage and Tudor in music, Merce Cunningham in dance, to name but a few. And this was the most exciting, self-confident and productive period of Olson's life. As he moved into a position of power in the college, he took command of his own voice as a poet. The *Mayan Letters* and the beginnings of *The Maximus Poems* came from this time. He was like a gigantic spring, bound tight ("the ball still snarled"), primed to unwind—and as he unwound, the energy poured out. An evening with him was an endless night of eating, talking, drinking beer, talking, eating—all the appetites and energies at work.

It is hard to tell whether he himself knew that in making the college, in replacing the old guard with the avant-garde, he was also wrecking it, as an ongoing economic entity. So strong was his confidence that, if he did know, it made no difference to him. He simply did what had to be done. It was one of those rare instances in the life of a poet of the external and internal man ripening together.

Later, when the college had closed, when it had died financially, he stayed on alone, to preside over the distribution of the physical remains, landlord of the detritus of his educational ideals. And of all those closely associated with the last bitter years, he seemed the only one immune to nostalgia. When the property was sold, to become a successful boys' camp, with that gloss of post-World-War-II affluence that he so hated in America—it didn't seem to bother him. He had done what had to be done.

He returned to Gloucester and plunged further into *Maximus*.

*

My own friendship with Charles was a winter-summer affair, blowing hot and cold. Our paths separated from time to time, but when they converged, it was not always smooth. He gave me a copy of his first published poems, a tiny pamphlet called y & x (Black Sun Press, 1950), which he inscribed, "For Paul and Nancy, early recognizers, now that the others are catching up." I became infuriated at the arrogance of this, felt that if I didn't protest, make some gesture, I would allow myself to be used endlessly. I wrote him an angry letter, and received an angry letter back in which he accused me of betraying him, of offering my friendship and trust, and withdrawing them. I felt at the time, and still feel, that I had made the right move: although this fight kept us apart for some years and established an edge of mutual suspicion that never disappeared from even our warmest subsequent friendship, I had maintained my own balance, kept myself from becoming fodder for his demands.

Charles could be ruthless in using people. He alienated Jonathan Williams at one time by referring to him as "one of the soldiers in my army." And when I had just returned from South America, he welcomed me to Gloucester, insisted on taking me out for dinner (though I doubted he could afford it), so that he could pump me on the trip, find out whether I had discovered anything he should know. Although both of us were in the best of humor, I again felt used.

There was a sort of megalomania that accompanied his size: he once told me that he might give up teaching altogether, perhaps give up writing, and go into "big business."

And he was proud, immensely proud, in other ways. When he was in grubby poverty, we would invite him for dinner, and he would always bring wine for us, or ice cream for the kids; and it was a battle gesture, not simple generosity. He would never allow himself to be

28

placed under obligation to another; and when, inevitably, such a relation became necessary, he was extremely reserved about it, even sharp at concealing it. When he had no money at all, and someone was supporting him, we never knew who it was.

His public appearances, as lecturer and reader, were often memorable occasions, his presence, his sense of the theatrical, his fine voice all contributing. But he could at times be extraordinarily arrogant, and at other times—or perhaps both at once—suffer oddly from stage fright. I know of two occasions when he threw out a listener at a reading, refused to go on until someone he decided he didn't like had left. ("You! Out!") And there were other times when he drank heavily before a reading, to overcome the terror. (Except for his last years, he was not generally a drinking man.)

If the distances were right, he was capable of a genuine empathy, a sweeping feeling for his fellowman. I saw him once at Black Mountain when he had returned from visiting the local Veterans Administration Hospital. He had been in the ward where a long row of beds were occupied by ex-soldiers, all black, all amputees. The concept of these black men spending the rest of their lives lying in those beds, with their chopped arms and legs, nearly overwhelmed him. "Jesus!" he roared.

There was something about people in large numbers that he was unable to deal with. He never liked New York City, was uncomfortable there, couldn't take the mass of it, couldn't find the handle.

But on Edisto Island, he met an ancient black man, Edward Simmons, tall like himself, to whom he responded immediately. Edward spoke a thick Gullah, and Nancy, a South Carolina native, had to interpret for Charles. They got along beautifully. Edward had spent his entire life on Edisto, with only an occasional visit to Charleston, forty miles away. Once he was taken to Columbia, the inland capital of the state. When he returned to Edisto, he asked, "Is there anything the other side of Columbia?" The remark delighted Charles.

Although Charles responded to a large number of friends, the terms of any relationship had to be just right: too close, too distant, too numerous, it just didn't work. He and my father, Harry Metcalf, were immensely fond of one another, and when Harry died, Charles wrote me a letter of condolence. It was a long, convoluted, involved thing in which he felt called upon to lecture on the cosmic meanings of death. The plain gesture—*he's gone, we loved him, we shall miss him*—that sort of simplicity was denied him. And, most sadly, at the end of his letter, he asked me to pass on his sympathies to my mother—forgetting that she was already dead, that he had sent me a letter of condolence, earlier, at the time of *her* passing.

At times, though, he was able to cut through complexities and cant with a marvelous directness. Clark Coolidge tells me of a television talk show on which Charles appeared. Charles hated television, only agreed to appear because they told him that Bill Russell, the great basketball player (six-foot-nine), would be on with him—he was furious when Russell didn't show. The commentator began to question Charles about the "inner meaning," the "deep significance," the "symbolism" of *Moby-Dick*, and Charles said, "Listen, *Moby-Dick* is a book about a man got his leg tore off by a whale."

*

Throughout his life, Charles—sort of like W. C. Fields—hated pets—dogs and cats—and only barely tolerated children, on his own special terms. And he was not the easiest husband or lover. He quite cavalierly abused all the obligations and privileges of domesticity. There is a poem written at Black Mountain (I thought it was in the *Maximus* series, but I don't find it there now) containing the great, galvanizing line, "Loneliness is a god damn lie!" That line, for me, more than any other single gesture, drew those of us who were his contemporaries together, introducing to one another "the islands of men and girls," shattering the meaningless rigidities in which we had locked ourselves. Duncan says that it was Olson who turned it all around for us, in the fifties, thereby making possible the entire modern (or "postmodern") movement in American poetry. If a single turning point, a single fulcrum can be chosen, that line is it. And it is the tragedy of his life, to me, that in his last years he was the loneliest of lonely old men.

He always envied me that I had a ballast in my life, other activities, lacking in his, to weigh off against writing. Twenty-four hours in every day, only so many of them he could sleep, and for the rest there was writing. And if the writing didn't come...? "You have been more commodious to yourself than I have," he said to me.

Nancy and I went to visit him in Gloucester shortly before he died, having no idea what his condition was. He was living alone, the apartment a worse chaos than ever. We took him out to lunch at the Tavern, and he allowed us to pay the check, a gesture to which he would never have submitted earlier. He was pathetic. He puffed desperately on a clay pipe that wouldn't burn—his answer to the emphysema that forbade cigarettes. His conversation rambled, and I was surprised to hear reactionary attitudes, anti-youth positions. He brushed his long, yellowy-gray hair. He spilled his water, and the waitress babied him.

Nancy and I left, badly depressed.

*

We didn't attend the funeral. In fact, I didn't know anything about it until some time after, when Nick Dean called. "Have you heard about Olson?" No, what about him? "He's dead."

I understand a number of his friends gathered at the cemetery for the service . . . and then repaired to the Tavern . . . and sat down to become quietly and seriously drunk.

What else is one to do?

1974

The Maximus Poems: Volume Three

Recently—14 September 1975—I attended an open house held at Arrowhead, Melville's old home in the Berkshires, to celebrate the acquisition of the property by the Berkshire County Historical Society, and, in this genteel way, to put the arm on the members of the Society, and anybody else they could grab, to raise funds to restore the house to the condition it was in, exactly 125 years ago, to the date—14 September 1850—when Melville purchased the property. At age fifty-seven, I was one of the younger people there. We watched the overdressed and elderly, the quiet rich of the Berkshires, doggedly hefting their frames out of their Chryslers to lend their presence and perhaps their pocketbooks to yet another historic moment; we toured the house, read the posters each announcing a proposed restoration, with price attached; we chatted with the long-skirted, lapel-labeled hostesses (in order to read a name, you had to stare at a breast) and found everything from total ignorance to serious scholarship in knowledge of what they were talking about; we listened to the speeches over the public-address system, under the rented jonquil tent; witnessed the presentation of the latest inflated artist's edition of *Moby-Dick*; we gabbled under the great white pines on the becalmed green lawn, and admired the flower beds, tailored by the Berkshire Garden Club; we drank the pale yellow punchless punch, and nibbled the little petits fours; etc., etc. . . . and then I came home and reread "Letter for Melville 1951," Charles Olson's bitter, personal diatribe against the Melville Society, against all official organization of the celebration of Melville's work.

This occasion, at Arrowhead, was not self-serving in the sense that Olson saw the activities of the Melville Society (you meet and talk and publish on Melville, the department head takes note, and your salary improves); no one seemed to stand to gain, personally, from what occurred on this brisk and sunny September day. Rather it was, indeed, a historic moment, the great wheels of society turning and pausing for an instant at a new notch: these old crocks creaking out of their Chryslers, fixing their glazed eyes on the speakers—these people who had never read *Moby-Dick* and never would, wouldn't know spermaceti from Gelusil—come now to put their seal of approval on this acquisition (for a hundred thou), restoration and preservation (another hundred and twenty-five thou) of the Great House where the Great Man wrote the Great Book.

Olson wondered about the meeting of the Melville Society in 1951—what would Melville think? But I wonder today—what would Olson think, about this occasion? And this leads at once to—which Olson? The angry young man of 1951 (he was barely forty then)—this strong, angry, bitter, somewhat paranoid but supremely confident young man who was single-handedly taking on the Melville Society in defense of the dead man they presumed to celebrate—and through them, ready to take on society at large? Or are we talking about the later, ingrown, Gloucester-obsessed older man—the man whose politics, whose political confidence, had by then turned to water—the man who wrote *The Maximus Poems: Volume Three?*

*

There is a type of American, several in the forefront of the arts, who believed throughout their lives that the Golden Age, in at least one place and time in the past, really did exist and who offered this as evidence of the Perfectibility of Man. These beliefs are often irrational and simplistic, and seem to coexist, in oddly good health, with an otherwise vast and cynical range of intelligence and erudition—the two areas of the mind somehow balancing each other. Pound felt that if he could just sit down and talk with Roosevelt for half an hour, explain the world to him, the international Jewish conspiracy, etc., Roosevelt would quickly see the light, change his approach accordingly, and the world would thereafter move forward on its proper course . . . and Pound was profoundly disappointed and frustrated when he couldn't even get an interview with Roosevelt. Charles Ives, who believed in the Perfectibility of America, based on some concept of the country derived from his childhood, simply couldn't understand why somebody didn't *do* something about Hitler . . . "why doesn't somebody talk to him?" Buckminster Fuller, whose descent from transcendentalist Margaret Fuller has left its marks on him, is a kind of scientific revivalist: the right use of the right technology will Save Us. And Charles Olson, the early Olson: the poem is an object in a field of force, is itself a force, with political potential.

This I take to be a Jeffersonian inheritance, and like so much else that Jefferson left us, it is deeply rooted in the American mind: the vigorous intelligence, often with vast accretions of knowledge, borne up, made buoyant, by a singular and anomalous naiveté. Jefferson believed in the Golden Age of Greece, and imported its forms, believed that forms could perfect modern American man. And Olson writes, near the beginning of *Maximus: Volume One*:

> one loves only form,
> and form only comes

33

                    into existence when
                    the thing is born

But, particularly in *Volume One*, Olson fluctuated between two
positions. The one:

            these things
            which don't carry their end any further than
            their reality in
            themselves

... things formally self-contained, endeavoring to be only
themselves, without political extension; and, on the other hand, the
possibility of the poem extending itself outward, as political
weapon:

                as the news that the almond
                was in bloom Mallorca
                accompanied the news
                that the book was in print
                which I wish might stop
                the workings of my city
                where so much of it
                was bred

And:

                                    the demand
            will arouse
            some of these men and women

And:

                    It is still
                    morning

It is this political faith, this faith in the possible political power of
the poem, that gives *Volume One* its early buoyancy. And the
passage, through *Volumes One, Two* and *Three*, is a record, among
other things, of the gradual loss of that faith.

This, the original faith, is Jeffersonian: the Grecian forms, the
architecture that Jefferson planted in the Virginia hills, peopled with
imported European professors and the bright youth of Virginia—that
was to be a practical factory leading to the Perfection of American
Man. (And then one reads of Edgar Allan Poe as a student at the new
university: the rich kids, sons of Virginia planters, with their
houseboys, their horses, their drinking and gambling, the cat houses

and moneylenders in Charlottesville.)

*

In *Volume One*, Olson addresses his readers, not as "dear readers" but as "fellow citizens"—or, at one point, "Ladies & Gentlemen." This is as we might be addressed from the White House. But elsewhere, he reduces his political range, becomes more realistic about his possible reach, and speaks to us as "you islands of men and girls."

*

> On ne doit aux morts nothing
>   else than
>   la vérité

. . . and, as throughout the poem, throughout all three volumes, whatever changes he may go through, whatever fluctuations between poles, one is required never to doubt that Olson knows precisely what "la vérité" is.

*

There was a strong element, in the Olson of *Volume One*, of what we call today "investigative reporter." He felt that merely by exposing what he called "conantry" he could reform Harvard; and he seemed to want to give the impression that this was just a beginning, beyond Harvard there was the educational system, and beyond that the whole American nation; and he looked to you, the reader, to see if you seemed to believe that he had that power, and if you gave the impression that you did, if the feedback from reader to poet was positive, then he shared that belief, and extended its range—much as politicians are reassured, fortifying their belief in themselves, by "pressing the flesh."

35

His obsession with history seems at times a corrective matter, almost mechanical, a realignment (tow and camber, kingpin and ball joint) so that henceforth the social machine will run according to its ordained design. As Don Byrd says, holding thumb and forefinger close together, "He was *that close* to being Jonathan Edwards."

Yet it was his political faith, and the buoyancy resulting from it, infusing *Volume One*, that energized him, and, in turn, energized American poetry, in the "postmodern" period of the fifties. As Duncan says, it was Olson who turned it all around for us.

But toward the end of *Volume One*, the faith begins to fail:

> ... give nothing now your credence
> start all over ...

*

Volume Two opens with continental drift, the Atlantic rift: a seismic disturbance in Olson ... which leads straight into the story of Merry and the bull:

> died as torso head & limbs
> in a Saturday night's darkness
> drunk trying
> to get the young bull down
> to see if Sunday morning again he might
> before the people show off
> once more
> his prowess—braggart man to die
> among Dogtown meadow rocks

Not that Olson was a braggart—or not that that is the point here—but that this is the first shift, the first major *rift*, in his front of confidence.

Symptomatic of this change is a turn to the land, which to Olson is feminine (and dirty), as opposed to the sea, which is masculine (and clean). There is the burial of Merry:

> Then only
> after the grubs
> had done him
> did the earth
> let her robe

36

                    uncover and her part
                    take him in

And:

                    the Sea—turn yr Back on
                    the Sea, go inland, to
                    Dogtown: the Harbor

                    the shore the City
                    are now
                    shitty, as the Nation

                    is . . .

Masculine, seafaring Olson is no longer putting out for fish, but
heading back to port, escaping disaster by mere luck (*Cashes*), and
dreaming of the woman envenomed by the snake, the woman fucking
the spirit of the mountain.

Not to belabor the psychological, but Olson himself says, in these
poems,

          a mother is a hard thing to get away from

. . . and he said to me once, in conversation, something to the effect
that concern or obsession with *rock* is psychological.

Note the venom with which he speaks, earlier, of the landscape at
Yellowstone . . . and, in these poems:

                    where moraine, and the more
                    evident presence of rock-tumble
                    gives the road, & center, its
                    moor character—moonscape
                    and hell)

                              *

Volume Two is the straddler, the linkage, the second act of a three-
act drama.

He speaks of drinking, the sailors who will not put out to sea, even
in fair weather, for drinking. It was somewhere around this point in
his life that Olson's own drinking increased . . . he started indulging
himself, whereas hitherto he had been abstemious—*that close* to
Jonathan Edwards.

                             37

*

In the poem *Maximus, at the Harbor*, he gets into the full conflict, sea and land, Okeanos and rock, male and female, man and woman:

> Okeanos rages, tears rocks back in his path.
> Encircling Okeanos tears upon the earth to get love loose,
>
> that women fall into the clefts
> of women, that men tear at their legs
> and rape until love sifts
> through all things and nothing is except love as stud
> upon the earth
>
>   love to sit in the ring
> of Okeanos love to lie in the spit
> of a woman a man to sit in her legs

... and ending with:

> The great Ocean is angry. It wants the Perfect Child

Later, there is mocking (as in the nesting records of the Mocking Bird):

> The Young Ladies
> Independent Society
> of East Gloucester
> has arisen
> from the flames:
>
> the Sodality
> of the Female Rule
> declared: We will Love
> with Kisses
>
> Each Other, and Serve Man
> as Our Child

*

Again, in *Volume Two*, he is no longer putting out for fish, the energy is in heading home for port:

> ... but the roar of this guy going through
> the snow and bent to a north easter and not taking any
> round about way off the shoals to the north but going
> as he was up & down dale like a horseman out of some
> English novel makes it with me, and I want that sense
> here, of this fellow going home

Arrived at port, little by little he slips into the Earth—presaging *Volume Three*. Not, as in the earlier poems, *placing* himself in Gloucester, but immersing, slipping, identifying himself, his own body, with the rocks, soil, gravel, contours, landscape, geography, geology, topography, in ever-narrower, more precise detail.

> and open an opening
> big enough for himself

At the same time, the division—Father-Ocean / Mother-Earth— becomes clearer, more exact:

> Mother Dogtown
> of whom the Goddess
> was the front

> Father Sea
> who comes to the skirt
> of the City

And later, he runs the two together:

> gardens ran
> to the water's
> edge ...

There is also a concern, through *Volume Two*, and reaching a climax in the next-to-last poem, with the River: the fresh water, flowing out of the Earth, invaded by the tides of Ocean, carrying the Flowers, on the outward tide, out to sea.

And, the final poem, a sort of decision, a decision we don't quite believe, a little thumbtack on the map of himself, his own tides:

> I set out now
> in a box upon the sea

*

39

Finally, there is *Volume Three*, of which this essay is presumably a review:

A View, in the Mirror, of Myself,
Age 52

This is a turning point, the pivot on which a revolving door revolves—or like the fishing boats he describes earlier, in the storm, anchors dragging, some slipping past the others, others crashing: Olson/Olson.

There begins, now, to be a drawing in, a concern with his own physical self: there is the poem titled "Maximus to himself June 1964":

And my arm
on my own body,
my own hand

mine

And:

not even able to get off into the land except
twisting
like the hair
from my own pubes

*

September 9, 1964: the poem about meeting Death. This was a little more than five years before his own death.

a stranger, suddenly
showing up, makes the very thing you were doing no longer the same.

*

We see, for the first time, a terrible, searing loneliness:

police cars turn my corner, no one in the world
close to me, alone in my home where a plantation
had been

40

... and we are thrust back to a line from the very earliest stages of *Maximus*, a line written and later cut (he read it in a public reading at Black Mountain College, but it is not in the printed version): "Loneliness is a god-damned lie!" We recall being addressed, in *Volume One*, as "fellow citizens," "Ladies & Gentlemen" and "you islands of men and girls," the sweep of the arm, gathering us in, turning it all around for us (as Duncan says), a political gesture; and one is reminded that politicians are *never* lonely.

More and more, the images in *Volume Three* are of *completion*:

<blockquote>
the earth
is only round when water
fills up ocean to the
top
</blockquote>

And:

<blockquote>
all that one cares for
proven

and come true
</blockquote>

But *in*completion is his natural state, and will not be that easily buried (see *Mayan Letters*, his admiration for the Maya, "the ball still snarled"). Angrily, bitterly, the incomplete returns: "Has March now been added so I have to live a 2nd month / of fear & Hell each year?"

Earlier, the exigencies of incompletion exhilarated him—but it is now all too painful, and he escapes to another completion: the candid identification of himself with his father, thereby completing the cycle that began back in the 1940s: see *The Post Office*, and the quotation at the beginning of *Call Me Ishmael* ("Loke, fahter: your sone!").

<blockquote>
My own
was so loaded in his favor as in fact so patently
against my mother that I have been like his stained shingle
ever since   Or once   or forever   It doesn't matter   The love I
learned
from my father has stood me in good stead
—home stead—I maintained this "strand" to
this very day. My father's   And now my own
</blockquote>

It can be said that all of *Maximus* is the exposition of a stance, a position in relation to the world, that was fully taken, and exists in its most compact form, in his earliest writings, back in the forties. (This is an attractive approach to many writers, for example, Joyce: was anything essential or substantial added, subsequent to *Dubliners* [even the title says it all]?)

This same poem, the one dealing with his father, ends in a crazy circular faint reprise on his earlier secular confidence (I won't attempt to copy the wild layout, on this page):

> as Your son
> goes forth to create Paradise
> Upon this Earth
> Secular Praise
> of You and the
> Creator
> Forever
> And an End to Hell

Later:

> Scene: I said to my friend my
> life is recently so hairy honkie-
> hard & horny too to that ex
> tent I am far far younger
> now than though of course I am
> not twenty any more, only
> the divine alone interests me at
> all and so much else is other-
> wise I hump out hard &
> crash in nerves and smashed
> existence only

And:

> in loneliness & in such pain I *can't*

And:

> off-shore out the Harbor for the 1st
> of all the nights of life I've lived upon,
> around this Harbor I hear also
> even in the fair & clear near round
> & full moon August night the
> Groaner *and* the Whistling Buoy in their
> soft pelting of the land I love

Lonely, painful, personal—signals of the nakedly emerging

romantic poet:

> Full moon [staring out window, 5:30 A.M. March 4th
> 1969] staring in window   one-eyed white round clear
> giant eyed snow-mound staring down on snow-
> covered full blizzarded earth after the
> continuous 4 blizzards of February March   5 feet
> of snow all over Cape Ann (starving
> and my throat tight from madness of isolation &
> inactivity, rested hungry empty mind all
> gone away into the snow into the loneliness
> bitterness, resolvedlessness, even this big moon
> doesn't warm me up, heat me up, is *snow*
> itself [after this snow not a jot of food left
> in this silly benighted house   all night long sleep
> all day, when activity, & food, And persons]
> 5:30 A.M. hungry for everything

If we take as the definition of the classical writer the one who
objectifies his material, pushes it outside the self, presents it in some
inherited or given pattern . . . and the romantic is the one who infuses
into his material as much of the self as he can manage, the forms
dictated by every idiosyncratic ripple of individuality, his material
virtually a sexual partner, into whom he must plunge all! all the body!
all the self! . . . then, by these definitions, the progression of
Maximus is from Charles Olson, the man who started writing about
Gloucester when he was in North Carolina, to some extent
objectifying it, and who told me, when he moved back to Gloucester,
he was nervous about the move, uncertain he could get *at* Gloucester
when he was that close to her—from such a man, the progression is to
the *Maximus* of *Volume Three*, who is utterly identified with and
infused into Gloucester . . . a man who becomes the Last of the
Great Nineteenth-Century Romantics.

> little aluminum masted cat boats were glinting
> in recently settling sun behind my yellow sweater over my
> non-Buddha non-healthy American-nerve Golden Triangle sensitive
> back between and below shoulders

And:

> looking up through my back & to topknot
> of Head to
> the eye of the apex of the bowl of the
> sky

43

. . . Seeing Gloucester—reality—through his body, his body become eyes, and reality—Gloucester—determined by the position of his body. This is under control, but it is not far removed from the kind of out-of-control experience that Theodore Dreiser went through as a young man—alone, lonely, broke, in New York, sitting alone in his room or standing, isolate, on a street corner, he would have to effect a circle, turn completely around, 360°, in order to bring himself into line with something, to align himself—perhaps with himself.

*

Near the end, the penultimate poem is like death and rebirth, the opening lines an act of self-burial:

> I live underneath
> the light of day
>
> I am a stone,
> or the ground beneath
>
> My life is buried,
> with all sorts of passages
> both on the sides and on the face turned down
> to the earth

As though having attended his own funeral, spoken his own brief eulogy, he finally *gives up* on this life, this people, this Gloucester, this America—gives up, and aims, vaguely, for the next:

> the initiation
> of another kind of nation

Finally, the last poem—the ultimate thumbtack on the chart of his life:

> my wife   my car   my color   and   myself

Olson/Olson: glimpsing himself in the mirror, he turns away, and climbs into the earth—or, to use a self-image from this volume, he is the crazy mole, spinning on the highway, and he takes an oar from the back of his car and lifts himself off the tarvia, into the marsh . . .

1976

Nancy and I recently—4 and 5 August 1980—paid a visit to Gloucester. The ostensible purpose was to meet and spend some time with that neglected poet Vincent Ferrini—a man both abused and loved by Charles Olson, and a man who, despite the gratuitous abuse, is now devoted to Olson's memory.

In "Letter 5" of *The Maximus Poems*, Olson tells Ferrini "you are more like Gloucester now is than I who hark back to an older polis"; he brags that he (Olson) is "not named Maximus for no cause," and finally dismisses Ferrini as "you who come after." Ferrini was angered and hurt—but, although several of his friends wanted to make a public issue of it, he was able to quiet them.

To understand Olson's motives, it is best to put his attack into historic perspective. *The Maximus Poems* was started at Black Mountain, and when the college folded, and Olson finished his duties presiding over the remains, he returned to Gloucester, settled in, and focused his energies on the poems. I don't know just when "Letter 5" was written—either before or after Olson returned to Gloucester— but in any case, Olson returns to Gloucester and finds Ferrini, Gloucester poet, already there . . . and The Big O, all six-foot-eight of him (he had been raised, remember, an only child) simply had to sweep the decks clean . . . there could be no competition.

Some time later, Olson gave a lecture at Berkeley. I don't have the text in front of me, and can't verify the wording, but Ferrini tells me that Olson said something to the effect that "Ferrini writes nothing but shit." Sitting on the beach the other day, at Brace's Cove, Vincent tells me, "Well, I felt like I'd just been knocked clean out of the arena." The double blow—left-right combination—first in "Letter 5" and then in the Berkeley lecture, was almost too much for him. But however he may have smoldered, he developed a curious defense, which became a subtle but not unkindly counterattack: he began writing a long series of poems in Italian-American dialect. By retreating to his ethnic sources and regrouping with those specific energies, he had created for himself an arena where Olson could not get at him!

Olson was Swedish-Irish. The great majority of Gloucester fishermen are Italian. I remember the time Olson took me down to the docks one day, to jaw with his "buddies" the fishermen. The men paid him barely polite attention—and then ignored him, began to speak among themselves, in Italian. Olson was miffed, and we departed.

This Ferrini, he was not only a Gloucester poet, he was, like the fishermen themselves, Italian. (The race that produced Dante!) Was that cause for resentment?

At the beginning of this essay, I referred to Ferrini as "that neglected poet." The judgments that critics wish to make about Ferrini's poems, their qualities and virtues, are one matter. And of course almost all poets are neglected—it comes with the trade. But the neglect I'm concerned with here is that afforded him by so many serious Olson scholars. I don't see how it is possible to come to an understanding of Olson without dealing, centrally, with his *amo/odi* relation with Ferrini.

Vincent has his own version, his own definitions, of their respective roles. In a letter to me, he writes: "Olson spoke to the intellectuals and the academic world, I speak to the non-poetry reader, the man in the street"; and elsewhere he writes: "the scholars scavenging Olson's big bang / the provincial mute catching up on my slang." Of course, nothing can be that simple, that clean-cut. In fact, the relation between "natural man" or image-seeker in *both* men is complex and fascinating, central to the study of both men, and well beyond the scope of this essay. But one point seems clear: lacking Olson's range or flamboyance (choose your term), Ferrini, almost (but not quite) without effort, was and is the man that Olson tried to be and wanted to be and to some extent was able to be—that is, the native, the man whose worldview originated in, whose eyes looked out to the world from, the city of Gloucester. (It should be mentioned, I suppose, that neither man *is* a native of Gloucester, Ferrini coming from Lynn, Olson from Worcester.)

Ferrini believed, and believes, in the Power of the Poem:

> do you think this moment
> after reading this
> you will be the same again

It is my contention that the Olson of the early Maximus poems shared this belief, and drew from it major energies; and that the poems thereafter are, among many other things, a record of the gradual loss of that belief, a gradual draining of those energies. But that, too, is beyond the scope of this essay.

46

While in Gloucester, we got in touch with Linda Parker, who occupies Olson's old apartment, 28 Fort Square. She had company, and lots of food—fresh Gloucester flounder—and invited us all for dinner. Ferrini was nervous about going; he had tried only once before, since Olson's death, to visit that apartment, and had been unable to stay . . . the spirit of that man who had so abused him, and whom he so deeply loved and loves, overwhelmed him. But this time, after ten years, he was able to stay, felt comfortable.

Linda runs a seaweed business, and the stuff was all over the place, outside and in. Generally, the apartment looked even more cluttered and raffish than when Olson was there. But we crowded around a big table, the flounder was delicious, the salad rich, we had brought homemade bread, there was ground sesame-seed-and-seaweed for the fresh local corn, and the wine was from everywhere.

Vincent talked comfortably and easily, as we all did—of Olson, poetry and life. If The Big O was present that evening, the mood of his ocean was benign.

1980

11

Where Do You Put the Horse?

"Sometimes I have the feeling that Metcalf is asking too much of the reader, that we must almost BE him to appreciate his work fully. In fact he is asking no less than this of the reader: change the structure of your mind."
Douglas Macdonald, proprietor, Two Hands Bookstore, Chicago.

As the subject of this remark, I guess I am both flattered and disturbed.

As a boy, growing up in Cambridge, Massachusetts, I used to eat something called an "Educator" cracker. And I think that's a fine and appropriate comment on that one-industry town where education is everything and where the educators, descendants of transcendentalists who were themselves descendants of Puritans, went about their daily business with a vigor aimed at no less than changing the structure of the student's mind.

Beyond school, I was exposed to—and learned to resist bitterly—other reformulators of my consciousness—not the least of whom was that modern version of New England hellfire and damnation, Charles Olson.

So, to find myself thrown into this group—standing in the pulpit, pointing an accusing finger—"You can't understand THE TRUTH until you restructure your mind"—it's a role in which I'm not comfortable.

I *am* at ease, though, to find myself following a path more or less of my own making, often isolated from those with whom it would be easier for me to join, people who nevertheless seem to follow certain directions and respond to certain assumptions that I cannot share.

These directions and assumptions are complex, not always

uniform, but there are certain common denominators.

*

Not long ago, that clever journalist, Tom Wolfe, wrote a magazine article called "The 'Me' Decade" in which he pointed out that the period since World War II has been one of unprecedented affluence in this country, with money pouring into all class levels, one of the results being a national obsession with self-improvement, the alchemical dream being "changing one's personality—remaking, remodeling, elevating, and polishing one's very *self* . . . and observing, studying, and doting on it (Me!)." He cites Bergman's *Scenes from a Marriage* as a typical Me-Decade film: over three hours of two people trading off: "I'll let *you* talk about *you* if you'll let *me* talk about *me.*" A sort of adult version of "I'll show you mine if you'll show me yours." And he quotes Alexis de Tocqueville: "Not only does democracy make each man forget his ancestors, it hides his descendants from him, and divides him from his contemporaries; it continually turns him back into himself, and threatens, at last, to enclose him entirely in the solitude of his own heart."

So we have all classes of Americans, particularly that vastly and only recently enlarged middle class (filled with sons and daughters of the downtrodden proletariat of the thirties), with newfound leisure and affluence—indulging, absorbing themselves, in ME: Synanon, Esselen, Arica, est, analysis, lemon sessions, scientology, encounter sessions, Jesus-freaking, consciousness-raising, clearing, rolfing, women's liberation, gay liberation, primal scream theory, Noetics, ESP, TM, pot and acid, Moonies, swapping & swinging, orgasm, orgone, Zen, Tao and mantras . . . and poetry.

*

The world is aflood with poetry. Guy Davenport has remarked that literature used to be a river flowing between banks, now it's a river flowing through an ocean. Vast numbers of Americans, striving to define the self by immersion in the self, emerge as poets. And as

49

obsessively interesting as the self can be, these poets nonetheless feel the need to join one another—not a true herd, but a kind of shared narcissism. Each group or school begins to develop and share certain cultural referents: the books read, the pictures on the wall, the jazz or classics on the stereo. And they begin to write poems about poetry, about being a poet, about writing poems . . . and the poems become filled, not with life observed, experienced and celebrated, nor with the peculiar idiosyncratic nature of the author, but with the group-shared cultural referents: Coltrane, Kline, or Creeley, whatever is current.

The poet ceases to speak in a personal voice, to speak out of himself or herself, but rather of what he or she has *learned*: they are poems of education, rather than of the authentic self.

And the sad part is that the original motive—to define oneself following absorption in oneself—is absolutely defeated: the poets quite simply become anonymous, all that they share rendering them impersonal.

The poets gather and hold "open readings": "I'll listen to yours and applaud, so that you'll listen to mine and applaud"—a social contract. They get grants to support themselves. And they are very "supportive" of one another.

The river flows into the ocean . . .

*

Some years ago, when I was young and impressionable, a knowledgeable academic said to me, "There are two interesting things in the world—integration and disintegration—and they are equally interesting." My response was the nineteen-thirties equivalent of "Wow!"—I felt that I had learned everything worth knowing, if I could just hold onto this formula.

More and more, I have come to realize how wrong it is. Integration and disintegration are *not* equally interesting. Pathology is *not* as interesting as health, the journey to chaos is *not* as interesting as the journey to order. The poet may—in fact *must*—plunge into disintegration, pathology, chaos, maintaining as best he can his own freeboard, his balance—but it is the return to the surface, the return to sanity, where the experience may be recorded, that confirms our

50

interest. Ishmael *survived* the sinking of the Pequod.

Most people's personal souls, my own included, are a rat's nest, and I find them just plain dull. My own approaches to history are very similar, another kind of dive into the soul: "I would think of history—and the varieties of language that ride with it—as a vast resource, into which one plunges with energy, comparable to sexual energy, demanding and focusing all one's vitalities. Following this, there is the second phase, which I learned absolutely from the poet Charles Olson: History is important only insofar as it impinges on the present. First, the plunge, the descent into hell, the near-drowning, if you wish; then the return to the surface. Because, if you drown, who cares? And if you don't plunge, who cares?" Two of my books—*Patagoni* and *I-57*—follow this pattern explicitly: the plunge into the past, and the return—the final chapter in both cases being a journal, a recording of the present.

It is precisely at this point that I part company with so many of my contemporaries. To them, the plunge—into one's personal soul, or whatever—is all there is, there is not even a thought of emergence, of return. And that's the tip-off, that the poet is in fact playing a kind of game: he's not *really* going to hell, he's not *really* going nuts—because if he were, the instinct to sanity, inherent and deep in all of us, would be disturbed and come into evidence.

But because it's a game and rules can be formulated and recognized, it gains support from the arts councils and foundations, all the officialdom of the arts.

Poetry, as a game, is much less interesting than baseball because it pretends to be concerned with such things as Truth and Beauty and the Soul, whereas baseball is explicitly a game, never pretends to be anything else, and therefore has direct and uncluttered appeal to our emotions.

*

Much of this so-called personal poetry is not really personal at all, in that it reveals nothing of the authentic self, or reveals qualities and materials most common and repetitious amongst us. And it is curious that this kind of poetry is apt to be decorated with—and numbed by—shared cultural referents. The urge toward the personal becomes, in fact, the very opposite of itself: a drive to anonymity.

It is difficult to write good baseball fiction because baseball is itself a fiction, and you're trying to build a fiction on a fiction. By the same token, and for the same reasons, it is difficult to build a poem on cultural referents.

*

I don't believe, as Douglas Macdonald suggests, that I am asking the reader to "change the structure of your mind." I do believe that the most interesting journey is the one from chaos toward order, that it is best enjoyed in good health, and that the whole trip will be most commodious for all concerned if, initially, the horse is placed in advance of the cart.

Is this so radical?

1979

12

Theodore Enslin

The Country of Our Consciousness, Etudes, In the Keeper's House,
and *Views.* By Theodore Enslin.

Over the years, and particularly in these books, Enslin has developed
a form peculiarly and accurately suited to his condition and
process.

In traditional poetry, indented lines carried material of secondary,
supplementary or supportive weight—as in Shakesperian "asides."
Enslin juggles with this method, at times indenting, to different
degrees, more than half the lines of the poem, at times sharpening the
breaks, at other times letting the material flow through as though in
spite of them. In this way, tantalizing tensions are established in the
interplay between and among lines. It is like watching a school of fish
in partly opaque water, the action shimmering just beneath the
surface:

> If I
> > knew nothing
> about it—
> > > that the Reach
> and Bay
> > lie close
> at hand—
> > > I would know this:
> A sea meadow
> > > and upland—
> brown,
> > thin boned
> like a fisherman's arm
> extended
> > hauling in lines.
> (The flash of sinuous fins
> too.)

and:

> A clean wash
> >   again
> water flowing
> >   over water
> created
> >   insubstantial
> as the mist
> >   which draws
> it up.
> >   Plunges
> >   down.

Accurately suited, because the method is the active arm of the man's condition, a constant sharpening of tools defining self-location, a shimmering refining of position: Enslin-to-Enslin—Enslin-to-wife-and-child—Enslin-to-place, immediate and beyond.

Always, as in the above-quoted poems, he manages to avoid a mechanical dichotomy—although at times he is tempted. As something of a recluse, a country man, he is tempted to submit himself to the "rightness" of Nature, at the expense of his humanity:

> to weed out
> or to put in
> weed of the foot
> planted
> where no foot
> was . . .

But the misanthropy, so common in this stance, never develops. Rather, he uses his relationships with Nature to work through to his humanity, reducing himself at times almost to a condition of stasis:

> It's a hard morning
> in which
> to do anything at all
> about nothing
> at all.

and:

> A wavering —
> >   still tenuous —

                not a breeze,
                            or yet
                more than the slight
                                movement —
                a curtain in this room.
                                It stirs,
                and that is life.
                                It stirs.
                Trembling,
                            (which stirs me)
                I am aware of it,
                                but not
                (yet) whence it came
                                    or
                where it is going, or
                                if it is cold,
                (the shudder)
                                or life
                within dark
                            secret places.

Not stasis, however—rather, that slow and only condition in which
things or people can be or become themselves:

                    And if the flower
                    flowers
                    let it by all means
                    in itself
                    flower.

Humanity, without coercion, from which he shrinks:

                    I would write you a letter
                        only
                    I know
                    the demand
                        a letter makes
                            something
                    outside of us
                        news which would
                    make us
                        or try to
                    you know
                        coerce.

Nevertheless, a man with passion:

55

You say:
> "I fear a man obsessed."
And I fear one
who is not.

One of the poems, "The Quarrel," brings together as well as any the accuracy of observation—Man/Nature—with accuracy of observation/participation—Man/Woman:

> It falls between us
> often I have
> seen a fleck of ash
> > fall
> gently held in air
> until
> > it settles
> black
> > and final
> on the snow between
> this tree
> that stone.
> It has no part of us —
> yet
> > it colors all we say
> or see and
> we will claim it
> darkening the dark
> or lightening
> > the light —
> in each a separate
> despair.
> > A catch of breath:
> It falls between.
> It is no thing of ours.

*

Given his abilities, his predispositions, it is not only natural but inevitable, his interest in homeopathy. One would say, like cures like, but the word *cures* is not accurate, implying as it does a process, where what exists in Enslin is more an identity, the tools defining self-location have become that sharp.

56

*

He is a literate, well-read man, anything but primitive. The simplicity at the core of his work is a difficult and sophisticated achievement.

Simplicity, perhaps, is not the word ... rather, sensibility, accurately tuned, whose circuitry may be assaulted, as in "A Sudden View":

> Hits me —
> knocks at
> the breath —
> goes deep
> somewhere inside
> as if
> something were broken.
> Won't do
> to say:
> It strikes —
> more than that.
> I forget what it was —

or overloaded, as in "A View in the Dandelions":

> Full bloom —
> miles of
> full bloom
> the eye
> revolts —
> dances in such heat —

and:

> I break open
> at the point
> where the door slammed.

There is another word that comes to mind with Enslin: *self-effacing*. (Typically, in the photograph, his eyes are averted from the camera.) But that too is ambiguous. The self nowhere forces its face upon you, but it is there, integral, just beneath the surface. He asks you to act as he has: to open your eyes, open your ears. Stop—look—listen. And he may not be gentle:

> The face

57

                              averted
              becomes
                        the edge —
              a sword-face
                                cutting and
              without pity
              against the air
              which takes it —
              re-forms
                        behind it —
              face
                    and refaced.
              The aversion
                              always
              removes
                        without departure —
              a haunt.
                        Defaced.

Perhaps self-effacing *means* integral. He is there, his integrity requiring no additives:

              Ah!
                The kindness
              of moments
                            is in the moments,
              not something added to them.
              It will not be separate
              or apart from them,
              nor from itself.
              Complaint of days —
              that bitterness is ended:
              It is the sap
                            sweet
              in itself.
                        But taste the day.
              You will see.

Shimmering in the partly opaque waters, he is to be reached only with appropriate difficulty:

              Do not crush my hand.
              Strength will not grasp it.
              Deceit will not reach it.
              Giving me the
                            'glad hand'

I would rather take
                    morose
aloofness.
            What you cannot say,
and what you will not.
Your hands in your pockets.
Years later
        the elements
— yours and mine —
will make the embrace.

1976

13

Guy Davenport

Tatlin! By Guy Davenport

One of the first instincts a reader experiences in discovering a voice as original as Davenport's—the voice speaking in the idiosyncratic mode of these stories—is to make connections: of whom does he remind us, what category can we open to admit him without over-straining ourselves? An obvious answer is Jorge Luis Borges. Having made this connection and restored ourselves a measure of comfort, we are then ready for the second step: how does he differ from Borges? And it is in this step, the divorce following the marriage, that definition begins.

Earlier readings in Davenport, notably his long poem *Flowers & Leaves*, give evidence of a connection with the composer Charles Ives, and this suggests a more complex connection-and-separation: Davenport-Ives vis-à-vis Borges-Stravinsky. Borges, for all that he is an Argentinian, is essentially, like Stravinsky, a European. Ives and Davenport are unquestionably American.

As Americans, the latter two are *brittle*, i.e., they tend to separate, to isolate, to string out their concepts, rather than comfortably integrate them in the assured European manner. In so doing, they deny themselves the *heaviness* that audiences and readers find reassuring . . . but the stringing out is part of the American process, of searching, of a new country still forming, of avoiding heavy masses, of keeping doors and windows open.

I maintain that it makes no difference what *materials* are used: whether Borges is in the Mediterranean or on the pampas, whether Davenport is in Brescia, Lascaux or Holland—it is the way of working, the structure, the "trace in the mind," that certifies these distinctions.

Note Borges's fondness for the word "labyrinth," his uses of labyrinths in his stories. This, like topiary gardens, is a very European concept, the elements, the mysteries that they compose, compacted.

We Americans, on the other hand, tend to thread our mysteries like a string of beads, as in the unsatisfactory form of science fiction, the gimmicks extended on the naked scaffolding and careless texture of the meretricious novel; or as in the deeply felt, deeply thought, long poems—the particles chiseled, carved out, isolate—of Pound, Williams and Olson (as opposed to *The Waste Land*, which feeds upon itself); and here, as Davenport handles them: his erudition masking and balancing certain direct simplicities, as Ives's tonal complexities mask the hymns and marches, achieving through a wedding of history and imagination a separation of the particles.

There is a significant connection between two images from the world of electromagnetics, images used in one case by Pound and the other by Olson. Pound speaks of the poem as the "rose in the steel dust," and Olson describes the poem as a thing among things, that must "stand on its own feet as, a force, in, the fields of force which surround everyone of us." Both these images suggest particles in a state of chaos, drawn into shape through an act of imagination, but retaining their character as particles, distinct from one another.

The American dynamic, in their example, the historical dynamic, is the separation and exposure of the particles, spread out and shaping, all in one difficult process, seemingly contradictory but not so, and not to be easily congealed in the European manner—particularly in Olson's view, and Williams's—not brought together, but spreading and shaping in one gesture.

It has much to do with geography, this separation and stringing out: the superb succession of sexual images in "The Dawn in Erewhon" in this collection of stories emulates the landscape, constantly unfolding.

An example of an opposite writer, opposite to Davenport and his predecessors, would be Richard Grossinger. His is a city-head, all things connecting. He finds space, not in the land, but in the demonic, the occult, the cabala, in the tarot, in alchemy, in multiple quasi-religious philosophies, in science fiction.

Grossinger's violation of the rose in the steel dust, of the field of force, is vital: it is bleeding madras, Pound and Olson left out in the rain, the colors running together.

*

61

Europeans seek mysteries—insoluble, self-contained, often without real hope. Psychoanalysis is consummately European. But in those Europeans who took the physical step of uprooting themselves, crossing the Atlantic, spreading roots across the new land, a kind of disconnection occurred, a psychic disjointing; a window opened, of which they-we may have been scarcely aware. And it is this resource that Davenport is mining, in *Tatlin!* . . . not, as I said, in the subject matter, but in his way of thinking, his way of working.

I think his erudition is something of a joke—he is laughing both at and with us, inviting us to laugh with him. He is proud of his knowledge, I'm sure, as any erudite man has a right to be, but he hasn't let it spoil his sense of fun, of gamesmanship. He laughs, as I remember Indians laughing at me in the backcountry of Peru, simply because I was white, because I looked and talked so funny—it was open, human and attractive, I enjoyed being laughed at in that way— I was able, if I wished, to enter into it, to join them in laughing at me.

This spirit of fun is important to the success of *Tatlin!* As writers, whatever resource we can tap that provides the most energy is the one that is most valuable to us. And we are never so energetic as when we are having fun.

1974

Flowers & Leaves. By Guy Davenport.

There is a kind of American—Charles Ives, Ezra Pound, Carl Sauer and Francis Parkman come to mind—who, without conscious effort or gesture, seems to have the American land, American geography, history, what have you, the American experience, if there be such— this "thing," whatever—so imagined and ingrained in themselves, passing seemingly from the imagination into the physiology, that it emanates from the pores, in every expression of the language or music. As a corollary, or an unearned increment, there is in these people a curiously immediate link with the classical; and, although in the case of Pound this may be rather consciously exploited, this consciousness is not the essence, either in Pound or in the others, of this immediacy: it is rather a sense one has of the man being massively and simply comfortable with both worlds, the modern and the classical.

Guy Davenport certainly belongs to this family.

The long poem, *Flowers & Leaves*, was published by Jonathan Williams in 1966. I read it when it first came out, but I have not been back to it since. It was with pleasurable anticipation that I picked it up again the other day, because the feeling I had for it, notched, as it was, back there behind all the other reading I have done in the seven years since then, was—what? —well, a feeling of "warmth."

There are echoes in Davenport of the Greek classics, the Old Testament, the Far East, Adams and Jefferson—his background as rich and interesting as his foreground, the surfaces of his language:

> If my fork pitch up Yorick in the okra

—the language reaching out, gathering us in, with innumerable warmths:

> The story-tellers have honied minds,
> Sweet hives of hatching ups and downs.

He is, among other things, a poet of the seasons and of the soil:

> In seed time learn, in harvest teach, in winter
> Enjoy

—a poet of place (I am told he lives quietly, almost isolated, in Lexington, Kentucky, with an occasional visit to an old family home in Anderson, South Carolina), but never exclusively any of these, for he is too richly informed to be a "simple" man. Zukofsky says, "Poetry is information." *Flowers & Leaves* reaches us with all the multiplicity of that radiant pun. There is no holding back:

> The road of excess leads to the palace
> Of Wisdom

and:

> Prudence is a rich, ugly old maid courted
> By Incapacity

and:

> O marry two
> To marry one.
> Outdo, outdo,
> Or be outdone.

He reminds us that it takes courage to act only out of desire:

> Who acts without desire
> Is beauty's ruin and the plague of nations.

For all its background, its tapestry of information, the poem in no way comforts the ignorant young, who might wish to place it in a museum. There is nothing dusty about "her Eros in jockey shorts."

And having written the above, I read on in the poem:

> The young are more inarticulate than children.
> And the articulations of an ancient world,
> Where olive, athlete, girl with jug or Lydian flute
> Might mean everything, foreshadow all worthwhile,
> Is a mute history, distant, distant and lost,
> But in the hard twist of a violent time only.
> Go back, the summer has whispered, go back.
> Pindar had no tongue for his ear. Under shin guards
> And shoulder pads, helmet, and blue jersey
> He was merely a boy . . .

Guy Davenport happens to be a very erudite man, but, unlike the academics, he never wields his knowledge as a weapon to beat us. Instead, the doors are open. Excess, again, as opposed to that ugly old maid, Prudence.

There is that easy flow of classical and modern juxtaposition: Apollo and Daphne lead into

> Tennis shoes, white socks, swim trunks inside out,
> And her blue-striped bathing suit twisted and wet
> On great towels, the season's transmutation of style

—the flow of a poet comfortable in both worlds.

And as he crosses classical with modern, he can, within the framework of either, create powerful polarities:

He made the butt of the mast to put down roots
Which tapped and gripped the sea-bed, and locked
Them fast, and made the rigging an arbor of grapes

—and he knows that it is from just such polarities, the tensions resulting from their unresolving, that poetry is constructed:

Be still and look both ways, for April comes.

It is characteristic of him that he has little tolerance for youth:

The ignorant young . . . .
. . . .
Know neither work nor contemplation,
"Born tired," shattering energy

and:

Chief objective of the American people
Is to be amused. Human nature
Among the young takes war for granted.

The debt to Pound is clear, but there is a kind of harmony in Davenport that is lacking in Pound's rough edges. Perhaps he is to Pound as Braque to Picasso, in which case the comparisons no longer depend on absolute value, it is just a matter of inclination: they are all good.

And having written the above, I come now to the following lines:

Her lilac stole and mimosa frock
As in the discipline of Georges Braque
Alert in aristocracy, intelligent
As the drachma owl.

"The ignorant young," says Davenport. But buried within that youth is the delightful child, central to this poem:

This Surrey oak dream
Children climb to sleep
In air or in enchantment
Fast inhabit caves of leaves

—and Davenport celebrates this from the very opening lines of the poem:

Poppies at their knees, autumn in their eyes,
They stole through the wheat so fat, so brown,

65

As the wild sad odor of leaves steals inward,
A quietness, a gathered hush, a slyness of eyes,
And charm of voices half birdsong rang.

In part 4, "Fire, October, Eyes," we have the deft use of the clichés of America:

... what landlord of this sweet land
Set the hills which so proudly we hail

and:

... blizzard of gold
And chill Housatonic and the church
In the wild wood

—this is purest Ives—Ives's sacred and secular jingles, church and circus—in an intricate matrix. And this quickly becomes explicit:

Charles Ives in the shallow Housatonic meadows
Walks with Harmony his wife.

The thrust of this last section is all toward the modern, out of Greece into America, the juxtapositions—ancient/modern—are now dynamic, history driving them:

To Haydn and Charles Ives, to the steel plosives
Of the motorcycle, to the silence of the apples,
Word on word folded ...

and:

The sincerity of carburetors, the insolence of cats

—until, in the last few pages, the poem comes at us, roaring, with a burden of history, comic and sad, in variations on the language of Francis Scott Key:

Whose broad stripes and bright
Stars, through the perilous fight over
The ramparts we watched were so gallantly
Streaming! And the rocket's red glare.

It is memorable. And one recognizes that Guy Davenport is one of the few Americans living capable of entertaining so much of past and present, holding it in suspension, in balance, and then laying it out, in tapestried language, in a sustained 114 page poem.

Dig out the book. The flowers are fresh, and the leaves glitter in the autumn sunset. It's all gold. It's all good.

1976

14

Jacob A. Riis

Jacob A. Riis: Photographer & Citizen. By Alexander Alland, Sr.

So many thoughts come flooding in when one studies these pictures. First off, the importance of this: that Riis never thought of himself as a photographer, in fact speaks in a most apologetic way of his camera work: "I'm downright sorry to confess here that I'm no good at all as a photographer." All one's thoughts about debasing one's art, using it as a tool for political or other purposes, here fall apart. For Riis, the camera was precisely that, a tool that he picked up, used for a brief period of time, and then dropped (when he finished with them, the pictures were given minimal care—they were discovered, through the persistence of one man, years after his death). But, rather than "using art as a tool," the formula turns around: we have here, instead, evidence of the artist's need to feed his work from sources other than his art, his cultural tradition—to place at least one leg, rooting him, feeding him, outside the world of, in this case, photography.

Extending this, with Riis's work in hand and the facts of his life, one is made aware of the terrible fallacy of teaching *any* art, no matter what it is: that teaching will only solidify and institutionalize the manners of the bad, which the good artist certainly doesn't need. Unless he is extraordinarily lucky and finds a teacher who will feed him only *information* and otherwise leaves him alone, education will generally delay him. There is only the virtue of the man, the woman, the artist, and this is nothing that can be taught.

There is just this in these pictures: the purity, the dignity of Jacob Riis, the man—his ability to survive, without warping, his early experience in this country (which reads like Kafka's *Amerika*, and confirms, oddly, the vision of that lonely Czech), and convert that experience, his own life, into a crusade: and then the unassuming but forthright way he picked up that easiest and most dangerous tool, the camera, to serve his cause. And it was the purity of the man, the depth of his conviction, his strength—rather than technical training—

68

that forbade him to do lax work.

Riis, in his relation to his subjects—the downtrodden, the criminal, the outcast—adumbrates a later photographer: Diane Arbus. The work of both demonstrates that curious, disarming respect, warming in the subjects, the people photographed, for the creature behind the camera, the intruder, the memorializer. How do they *know* that he or she wanted to serve rather than exploit them? Even the cocky ones, mugging—Riis established something with them.

It is easy to categorize this as documentary photography, or photo-journalism, which is to miss the point altogether. No doubt Riis so intended and, to the very end, so considered it. But this work will stand with the finest of any place or time—and he had only the integrity of his own passion to instruct and guide him.

You students of photography, look at these pictures. Then put down your manuals and magazines and get away from that art school. Go out and do something *absolutely else*. If you are truly gifted, you are truly gifted—and little anyone can say will help or hinder you. If not, take a shot of the family at Christmas with your Instamatic—and for the rest of the year, leave it alone.

1975

15

Edward S. Curtis

The Portable Curtis: Selected Writings of Edward S. Curtis. Edited
and with an introduction by Barry Gifford. Foreword by
Theodore Roosevelt.

As inhabitants of the Land of Opportunity, Americans of humble
background—native-born or immigrant—have for generations been
obsessed with Education: Education as the key to open the door to
the nation's riches. And yet it is odd how often the truly valuable
work in this country has been done by people who bypassed the
universities, the formal bureaucracies, and went right to the work
itself: the amateur, the self-taught, his work authenticating itself in
the doing.

Edward S. Curtis had no training as a photographer—in fact, he
made his own first camera. Nor was he trained in anthropology . . . his
formal education terminated with grade school. Like Jaime de
Angulo, with whom there are other interesting parallels, he simply
went to live among the Indians, and his project, that was to obsess
and nearly overwhelm him, presented itself, growing, as he reached
into it, daily, monthly, yearly.

The question of ambition doesn't enter into it—he was too busy,
too engrossed in what was opening before him: no less than to study,
photograph, record, transcribe the mythology, ceremonies, religion,
history, language, arts, customs, daily life of *all* the tribes west of the
Mississippi, from New Mexico to Alaska—at the crucial time when
these tribes were dying, but when, through their older members, their
cultural wealth was still accessible.

Like de Angulo, Curtis discovered that he had an intuitive sense of
the Indian's nature. Unlike de Angulo, however, who associated
principally with one tribe of Indians, Curtis was called upon
repeatedly, as he moved about, to exercise this intuition, to generate
anew the confidence of his hosts and subjects.

This is, finally, the most interesting aspect of the work of all

70

portrait photographers, at least of those whose subjects are "strangers": this contract, this bond of trust, established between photographer and subject. Between Curtis and his Indians, between Diane Arbus and her freaks, between Jacob Riis and his New York criminals, there is an open way, an exciting passage of understanding, back and forth, revealing heart and character of both, photographer and subject.

Curtis spent thirty years on his project, almost without interruption, as long as his health and energy would permit. Initially hard-pressed for funds, he later gained the support of J. P. Morgan, and the Morgan estate, to the extent of over a million dollars. The resulting documentation ran to twenty volumes, including twenty-five hundred photographic images. These were printed in the most expensive and permanent manner possible, in an edition of five hundred, and sold at $3,000 per set—and even at that extravagant price they disappeared quickly, in rare book rooms and private collections. As a result, the recent excavation and exposure of the work has been an archaeological project in its own right.

We have already had editions of selected photographs, but the present volume, *The Portable Curtis*, provides a sampling of the writings, as well as images. Editor Barry Gifford has chosen to demonstrate the scope, the range of Curtis's interests, by giving us examples of every aspect of the work: Mythology, Ceremonies, Medicine and Medicine-Men, Religion, Historical Accounts, Arts, Warfare, Social Customs, Biographical Sketches, a Note on the Indian Music (by Henry F. Gilbert), Vocabulary and Tribal Summary.

It is a handsome, well-made book, absolutely essential to the specialist in western Indians . . . and a reader with only a casual interest cannot fail to be impressed with the range, energy and skills of this extraordinary man.

One final note, on the strange overlappings of our history: Edward S. Curtis lived on until 1952 . . . I was thirty-five years old then, and I find this fact, together with the fact that through this man I have a living link with our Indian heritage—I find this a little shaking.

1976

16

Paul Bowles

A Journey in Search of Bowles

Living in a rural area as I do, in presumably "cultured" Massachusetts, access to the books I want is not always an easy proposition. I have neither the funds to buy everything nor space in which to put it; even if I had both, much of what I'd like to read is quietly slipping out of print. In this subtle way the vagaries of the commercial market dictate what we read.

I could not, therefore, organize a systematic reading of Paul Bowles, taking the books, say, in chronological order. It was a question of taking what I could get, where and when I could find it: local public libraries, nearby college and university libraries, borrowing from a friend, the creaky interlibrary loan system, etc. The largest of the local libraries has a very efficient staff that seems to throw out anything over twenty years old. Fortunately, in some of the smaller libraries, the staffs are wearier or more negligent. And interlibrary loan here in Massachusetts may only mercifully be called a "system": I live in the western part of the state, and hardly ever will they cross that international boundary, the Connecticut River, to tap the riches of Boston and Cambridge.

This discourse, then, will be the journal of a random journey, the books appearing unexpectedly, around the bend, in the river of reading.

*

Collected Stories, 1979; *Their Heads Are Green and Their Hands Are Blue*, 1963.

To begin with a cliché: Most human life depends on the existence of some sort of community, and the function of a community depends on the fulfillment, in innumerable details, of a contract of participation by each and every member. Those who fall out, who refuse or fail to fulfill the terms of the contract, may be accommodated, at the expense of the rest, in asylums, prisons, hospitals, universities, art colonies, convents, government bureaucracies, the welfare rolls or the armed forces—all such institutions for the isolation of the socially incompatible. Up to a point—a point of numbers and expense—a healthy society can support and sustain these deviates.

In our darkest moment, an awful thought may occur to us: suppose *all* of us, whatever the extent of our participation in or withdrawal from society—suppose all of us were to refuse or fail to fulfill the unbelievable number of units of action and response that go to make up our daily contract with the world in which we live?

With appropriate horror we read in the newspapers of the death toll from accidents on the highway. But how many cars pass each other in close proximity at dangerously high speed on American highways, daily, *without* accident? Millions? Billions? Trillions? All because all drivers concerned are responding, over and over again, day in and day out, in a responsible way, to their (our) part of the social contract.

Suppose that response were suddenly to cease?

Paul Bowles's best tales and essays seem to begin from some supposition such as this. The Judeo-Christian mind—either as characters in the stories or as Bowles himself in the essays—comes up against the Islamic psyche, history, customs, manners, behavior—all of these so alien to his as to represent, and in fact precipitate, an utter breakdown in all the details, the units of action and response, of which the human contract is constructed.

Bowles quite naturally abjures colonialism . . . but the descendant of the colonial becomes a tourist, or as in Bowles's case, a permanent visitor—in search of the exotic, the un- if not anti-Western. And he surely found it. Consider:

> The difference between Mustapha and us is possibly even greater than it would be were he a Buddhist or a Hindu, for there is no religion on earth which demands stricter conformity to the tenets of its dogma than that supra-national brotherhood called Islam.
>
> Mustapha does not believe in the same good or evil as we do. Such personal concepts as continence and honesty, such social virtues as a taste for the "democratic way of life" and a sense of civic responsibility,

mean very little to him. He thinks of peace as that boring and meaningless interlude between wars, of democracy as a weak and corrupt substitute for autocracy. The best ruler is a benevolent tyrant . . .

. . . logic is the last thing to look for in Mustapha's behavior.

Although Mustapha may do what he feels like doing, simply because no other cause has suggested itself to him, he will almost never say what is in his mind. For, according to his devious reasoning, if he were to utter his true thoughts, he would be giving himself away, playing recklessly into your hands. Thus it is extremely important for him to make conversation which will lead you away from, rather than toward, whatever is in his mind or what he believes to be the truth.

"Only a fool tries to say the truth," they tell me. The more speculative ones will go off into a fancy and specious kind of argument according to which, since only Allah knows the nature of truth, man can scarcely take it upon himself to pass judgment as to what is true and what is false.

. . . it is a refusal to believe that action entails result. To him each is separate, everything having been determined at the beginning of time, when the inexorable design of destiny was laid out. All of life is a desperate gamble, and everyone has the odds against him. It is the most monstrous absurdity to fear death, the future, or the consequences of one's acts, since that would be tantamount to fearing life itself. Thus to be prudent is laughable, to be frugal despicable, and to be provident borders on the sinful. How can a man be so presumptuous as to assume that tomorrow, let alone next year, will actually arrive?

He has a passion for personal independence. He does not look for assistance from others; indeed, he is incapable of receiving it; nor does he believe in the possibility of one person helping another, since all aid comes from Allah.

If we read this as background for the actions of the Shah of Iran, abruptly thrusting his country into the modern Western world . . . it is no wonder that the result is regression to a fundamentalist, and subsequent chaos.

One is reminded of the conflict, here in America, between the white man and the Indian—a "perfect" conflict that was resolved only by the near elimination of one of the contestants. Is *that* what it takes?

Turning to the stories:

Those that take place outside Morocco—"The Echo," "Call at Corazon," "Pages from Cold Point"—turn on terrible domestic quarrels and separations. Broadly, though, the theme remains the same: whatever the effort toward human contact and community—

the human *contract—it will fail.*

With a clear head and remarkably good spirit, Paul Bowles tells us these tales of disaster and doom.

"Pages from Cold Point" opens with the thoughts of one of the characters, but one feels it is Bowles himself:

> Our civilization is doomed to a short life: its component parts are too heterogeneous. I personally am content to see everything in the process of decay. The bigger the bombs, the quicker it will be done. Life is visually too hideous for one to make the attempt to preserve it. Let it go. Perhaps one day another form of life will come along. Either way, it is of no consequence. At the same time, I am still a part of life, and I am bound by this to protect myself to whatever extent I am able. And so I am here.

Paul Bowles is here, in story after story—tales of violence, precisionlike failure, cataclysmic misunderstanding—as though any two characters were like two hands that are supposed to be clapping but instead wave cleanly through the air, missing each other with perfect madness.

Scattered among these tales of foreign lands are a few—"How Many Midnights," "If I Should Open My Mouth," "The Frozen Fields"—that take place, oddly enough, in the good ole U.S. of A. What is odd is how comfortably and well Bowles, the exile, writes about his native land, as though he had never left.

"The Frozen Fields" is written with persuasive clarity, a thoroughly "American" story. On the other hand, "He of the Assembly," which follows a few pages later, is drug mania, a kef fantasy.

Bowles is never a "wild man," nor does he ever despair, no matter how gloomy his tales *seem* to be . . . I say *seem,* because, no matter how hopeless the case, in every tale, he writes with such equanimity, skill-under-control, and even good cheer: despite the events, it is difficult to draw out despair when the reading is such a pleasure.

Up above the World, 1966.

After the essays and stories, this is an odd little book. Odd in that it appears so fragile, so undemanding, and—let's face it—commercial. A short novel, it can virtually be read in one sitting—because of its brevity, and because there is so little to arrest, to nail down our attention. The mind and eye fly forward, the fingers slip the pages . . . it is the sort of book one reads in airplanes, I suppose, and quite rightly so, because it is all consumed *in flight*.

True, there is one Bowles hallmark: "It seemed to help prove the truth of a suspicion she had long entertained: people could not really get very close to one another; they merely imagined they were close."

It is that old situation of absolute misunderstanding and mistrust that seems to characterize Bowles's view of society—the condition that Melville dealt with in such tormented fashion in *The Confidence-Man*—and that has since been homogenized and standardized as stock material for the "mystery" novel. (In this genre, it is blandly assumed, by author and reader alike, up until the very final page, that nobody understands anybody.)

So Mr. Bowles possibly was trying to replenish a diminished exchequer. A situation thoroughly understandable—and we forgive him.

The Sheltering Sky, 1949.

A response to this book is a question of one's attitude—several of which are possible.

First off, let it be said that this is a solid effort, far superior to *Up above the World*—deeper, more ambitious, more accomplished in every way.

But after that, what is it?

A major tragic study of the human condition, of modern existential man in the wasteland of his own creation?

A magnificent drama of the Anglo-Saxon in a doomed struggle with the Sahara? (By pure coincidence, I have been reading, at the same time, a story of the Donner party in California.)

An evocation of the implacable incompatibilities of two alien races?

A trio of Anglo-Saxon protagonists exploring-exploiting-luxuriating-suffering in their emotional-sexual-sociological entanglements—hyperliterate neocolonials indulging themselves against a backdrop of the stoic Arab-Islamic native?

Or is it, finally, simply, what is meant by the term *a good read*?

As one goes through the book, one's mind seems to shift uneasily among these attitudes—the attitudes themselves shimmering like Saharan hallucinations. (I imagine the fact that this simile suggests itself to me is a credit to the undeniable power of Bowles's writing.)

Still, always, there is Bowles's relentless, even-spirited pessimism—as in the case of the American women speaking of the Arabs: "Men were looking at her, but with neither sympathy nor antipathy, she thought. They had the absorbed and vacant expression of the man who looks into his handkerchief after blowing his nose."

Or the American man: "There were days when he felt contempt for these absurd people; they were unreal, not to be counted seriously among the earth's inhabitants."

At the end of the book, the very last lines, Bowles switches from the shell-shocked heroine to a passing trolley car: "At the edge of the Arab quarter the car, still loaded with people, made a wide U-turn and stopped; it was the end of the line."

The end of the line, perhaps, for white and Arab, but also a metaphor for the forthcoming end of the world: spaceship Earth, still loaded with people, will make a wide U-turn and come to a stop. When this occurs—and it will, at any moment now—Bowles's emotions will be powerful, but they will be controlled . . .

Let It Come Down, 1952.

This is an entertaining novel. This is a good novel. This is a sound novel. This is a well-crafted, well-written novel. This is a *good read.*

And if all this sounds like damning with faint praise—well, yes and no. I mean, literally, all-the-above comments; but there would be little else to say here if I had not first read *The Sheltering Sky*, experiencing the greater force of which Bowles is capable. In fact, these comments may well turn into a second, more enthusiastic review of the earlier novel; or, at least, a comparison of the two.

The meat of nearly all of Bowles's writing—the conflict between WASP and Moslem—represents a particular phase of sociology and history. In the course of empire, the expanding nation conquers the natives, imposes its laws and culture upon theirs, attempts, if not to eradicate the latter, at least to put it out of sight. The natives resist, then cower, yield, and eventually develop an elaborate system of strategems for maintaining their own world, semivisible but very much alive, beneath the cover of the conqueror. All this would date back to the nineteenth century, well before the phase of which Bowles is writing. However, although Bowles is writing of the mid-twentieth, his phase actually began back in the nineteenth, when some of the wilder, more colorful creatures, thrown loose from the tight societies of England or Europe, became intrigued with the "mysterious," the "exotic," and went native, living in tents with the Arabs, riding camels, smoking kef, etc. That fine poet, Janine Pommy Vega, who has much of this vigor and wanderlust in her own spirit, has made me aware of several nineteenth-century European women who would fall into this category: Isabel Burton, Jane Digby El Mezrab, Aimee Dubucq de Rivery, and Isabelle Eberhardt (whose book, *The Oblivion Seekers*, bears an introduction by Paul Bowles). There was something wild, wacky and wonderful about these people—an initial rush of energy, if you wish. But by the time we get around to the moderns of whom Bowles writes, these outcasts from the industrial world seem to be more a set of well-to-do dilettantes, driven, surely, as were their predecessors, but with a kind of cold, Anglo-Saxon control that renders the outcome sordid and decadent rather than exotic. Both novels, *The Sheltering Sky* and *Let It Come Down*, wind up with these characters having so mismanaged their lives—by design!—as to find themselves in near-suicidal predicaments in the implacable Moslem backcountry or Sahara. There is, now and then, a faint odor of an old cliché: the British imperialist in the jungle, quaking in his boots but not showing it, as he listens to the native tom-toms.

So much for the pattern of the two novels. But what is the difference between them, what is it that makes the earlier one, *The Sheltering Sky*, so much more powerful? One is thrown back to the most elemental questions, dealing with all the arts . . . what is it in a really superior work, a work that deals with a specific place and time, that both roots it forcefully in its matrix and at the same time lifts it out, throws it into the current of all our valued inheritance? There is a simple force in the principal characters of *The Sheltering Sky*, a force in accelerated revelation as the book nears its end, a force that overrides the ordinary decadence of these people, a force that lifts them into figures of significance beyond what their characters would seem to have earned—a force which, one feels, at its height, is straining the limits of their creator's control.

When a book is nearly out of the author's control—is this some sort of measure? As a generalization, I doubt it. But I think it may be important in the case of Bowles, whose cool, controlled pessimism in the best parts of this book, as in the best of the short stories, is momentarily but severely shaken.

Meanwhile, *Let It Come Down* is an entertaining novel. A good novel. Etc.

The Spider's House, 1955.

This is an entertaining novel. This is a good novel. This is a sound novel. This is a well-crafted, well-written novel. This is a *good read*.

The comments begin to become interchangeable. However, there are certain important differences between this and the prior novel. It is revealing in the ways that some of the characters serve as apparent alter egos for Bowles himself. The American, Stenham, with his soul-searching recall of his own peregrinations, backward through membership in the Communist party, through his parents' rigid and devout agnosticism, to, finally, some sort of very Christian-sounding notion of personal salvation—this has the ring of being Bowles himself. And there is the "final solution" for the American expatriate in Morocco: "It would not help the Moslems or the Hindus or anyone else to go ahead, nor, even if it were possible, would it do them any good to stay as they were. It did not really matter whether they worshipped Allah or carburetors—they were lost in any case. In the end, it was his own preferences which concerned him. He would have liked to prolong the status quo because the decor that went with it suited his personal taste."

The American expatriate in any exotic land.

But, more importantly, Bowles seems to have placed some of his own thoughts and values in the leading character of this book—Amar—who is, for the first time, not a WASP, an American, but a native, a Moslem. This is an odd gesture, considering Bowles's insistence on the absolute incapacity of the two races or religions to understand each other. He would seem to be attempting to cross a bridge here that he has told us repeatedly does not exist.

This is Amar the Moslem speaking:

> When the time came he always found it difficult to participate; he could only grin and be thrilled by the others. His friends had long ago given up trying to instill in him a sense of teamwork on the soccer field. His principal interest there was in the brilliance of his own plays. Sometimes they would ask him if he thought he were playing alone against both teams. When they complained he would say impatiently: "*Khlass!* Was that a good pass or wasn't it? Do you want me to play or don't you? Just tell me that much and then shut up."

The great baseball player, Ted Williams, was often accused of this. He would hit with men on base, or without men on base, there was no relevance, no connection between his performance and the needs of the team, the strategy of the moment. Furthermore, he was known as a misanthrope, remote from his teammates, often in trouble with the fans and the press.

To respond to the seductions of the team, to be a "money" player, one must consciously and willingly or not, share some faith in the possibilities of common humanity, be able to draw some strengths from outside oneself, from that pool of common human endeavor. And this, of course, a true pessimist, a true misanthrope, cannot do.

(It should be pointed out, though, that neither Bowles himself, nor Bowles-as-Amar, the hero of the novel, is a misanthrope. Pessimist, yes; misanthrope, no.)

There is another way in which this book stands out from the others: In delineating the incompatibility of WASP and Moslem worlds, there is a quality that is almost *prurient*. Repeatedly, relentlessly, Bowles demonstrates a fact of the American abroad: that we seek and find the worst, and are ourselves the worst when we are out of our own country. The American who abandons his own land is generally trying to confirm something unpleasant—hence his prurience—

something unpleasant about the world he finds, the world he leaves, about himself, life, what-have-you.

This is not to say that Bowles's writing is in some way unclean. It is not. It is remarkably, refreshingly clean, washed at its best with a marvelous, natural clarity. But he arrives at this cleanliness, as I have suggested repeatedly, by means of his implacable, cheerful pessimism.

There is a parallel, toward the end of the book, with Ralph Ellison's *The Invisible Man*. The Communists, posing as saviors of the oppressed, insinuating themselves into the confidence of the most articulate of the downtrodden, become, through the terrible abstractions to which they bow and the amoral behavior resulting, as alien to the native as the oppressor.

And, true to form, Amar, our hero, courted and compromised by both sides, American and Communist, winds up callously abandoned by both.

Nevertheless, this is an entertaining novel, this is a good novel, etc.

Next to Nothing: Collected Poems, 1926-1977, 1981.

These are clearly the poems of a novelist. The words that come to mind are: effete . . . ethereal . . . romantic . . . thinly lush. They remind one of poems written by an etiolated, fin-de-siècle gentility: "In the platinum forest walked a white maiden," etc.

At times, with his small formal inventions, he is tentatively an e. e. cummings. Because cummings was a poet, he pursued these inventions exhaustively; Bowles, as a novelist, does not.

There is also more than a little of that ultimate exfoliation of the romantic: surrealism.

What is the significance of the title, *Next to Nothing*? Is this Bowles's own opinion of the poems? In the prose, he is not an ego— and this is refreshing (this is one of the great virtues of a Bowles narrative: the author, as a personality, and his stories, his characters, are almost always in perfect balance); nevertheless, he is never self-effacing or falsely modest. One senses that the poems are tentative, that he felt less sure of himself in this mode.

The tone is so "elevated" that, reading them, one after another, one becomes almost lulled into a trance. Perhaps this is deliberate, perhaps Bowles thinks of poetry as equating that hypnotic consciousness derived from smoking kef.

Nevertheless, there is a gradual transition over the years. Beginning in the lofty and saccharine, they penetrate into the surreal, and along about 1940, there seems to be a tentative attempt to be more real, to involve direct meaning. They remain, however, skewed by the quality of the kef-dream—or by the self-conscious necessity to be "poetic"—whichever it may be.

It is not well known that William Faulkner wrote and published a volume of poetry, entitled *A Green Bough*.

> It was a morning in late May:
> A white woman, a white wanton near a brake,
> A rising whiteness mirrored in a lake . . .

Like I said, the poems of a novelist.

Yallah. Text by Paul Bowles. Photographs by
Peter W. Haeberlin, 1957

It was a fortunate accident that I came across this book right after reading the poems. It would seem that, through the medium of Peter Haeberlin's photographs, Bowles is able to achieve what photographs at their best do so very well: the making of a poetic statement with utter unself-consciousness. Perhaps some of Bowles's music does the same thing; I don't know, I'm unfamiliar with it.

The photographs are the geographical and human record of a journey taken by Haeberlin across the Sahara, north to south, from Algiers to Lake Chad. They are superb pictures, beautifully reproduced. The text is documentary, factual, and modest, providing appropriate information with minimal editorial comment.

By reaching out beyond language to this other medium, photography, Bowles is able to express to us his deep love for this area and its sadly changing peoples. It is a naked, lyrical statement that I think his own makeup would not allow him to make, in either poetry or prose.

82

Midnight Mass, 1981.

This, a collection of late short stories, is clearly an afterthought, and it is fitting that it came into my hands after most of the others. Although the impeccable craftsmanship is there, as always—one has the feeling this will never leave him—these stories add little to his stature. Nor do they subtract from it. They are simply there.

There is a moment, however, in one of the stories that does stick in one's mind. In "Here to Learn," Melika, the beautiful young Moroccan girl, born into ignorance and poverty, makes her escape through the agency of her lover, a rich American tourist. He takes her out of Morocco to Europe and eventually to this country and Los Angeles. They fly across the Atlantic at night and naturally this is her first experience of airplanes:

> Once again she saw nothing from the plane, but this time the journey went on for such a long time that she grew worried. Tex was sleepy, nevertheless she disturbed him several times to ask: Where are we?
>
> Twice he answered jovially: In the air. The next time he said: Somewhere over the ocean, I suppose. And he stole a glance at her.
>
> We're not moving, she told him. We're standing still. The plane is stuck.

This is a marvelous metaphor, both for the "native" thrust abruptly into the modern world and for the whole modern world itself, of jet speed and mechanization. At thirty-thousand feet and six-hundred miles an hour, "the plane is stuck." In a time warp.

Later, in Los Angeles, she observes the freeways: "The freeways inspired her with dread, for she could not rid herself of the idea that some unnameable catastrophe had occurred, and that the cars were full of refugees fleeing from the scene."

No comment.

Without Stopping: An Autobiography, 1972.

As I have been reading the works of Paul Bowles, the novels, stories and poems, I have been looking forward to this book, the auto-biography, with considerable anticipation. I knew little about the man except as he revealed himself in his work; and in a writer as controlled as Bowles, the revelations were never spectacularly clear. So I have been making guesses and assumptions about him, about his background, his life, his nature, looking forward to eventual verification.

But *Without Stopping* turns out to be such a disappointment, such an emptiness, that the whole project suddenly seems unimportant.

The early part of the book is interesting, the childhood, the origins, etc. He turns out to be the son of a Long Island dentist, who was a rather mean man, and whom he transfigured as an uncle in one of the better of the short stories, "The Frozen Fields." But the bulk of the work, once Bowles matures, is a gossipy Cook's tour—without stopping!—of exotic places to live and "interesting" people to know. The beginning, inevitably, is a trip to Paris, where he joins Gertrude Stein's salon. (How many writers have tried to climb this particular ladder to success? It must be the most documented and boring episode in American literary history.) What follows is an endless succession of travels and name-dropping—which the publisher celebrates in a massive back-cover blurb, all the famous names he has rubbed shoulders with. On pages 210-11, for example, we are treated to Henri Cartier-Bresson, George Anthiel, Father Divine, Gertrude Stein, Igor Stravinsky and Henry Miller—all on a personal basis.

It is hard to imagine how a man who can write as well as he does in *The Sheltering Sky* and the best of the stories could indulge in so much unrevealing personal trivia. One can only assume it must be for—money? (although he never seems poor)—or fame?—or, simply, notice?

One thing that does come clear in this book: I had not realized how much time he has spent in this country, particularly New York. He has not been a full-time expatriate.

And there are other moments, here and there, few and scattered, that catch one's eye: When he was a small boy, his mother said to him: "Did you ever try to make your mind a blank and hold it that way? You mustn't imagine anything or remember anything or think of anything, not even think 'I'm not thinking.' Just a total blank. You try it. It's hard." And the young Paul Bowles "began to practice secretly, and eventually managed to attain a blank state, although I was inclined to hold my breath along with it, which automatically limited its duration. Whatever powers of self-discipline I have now were given their original impetus at that time." Self-discipline—and control.

As a grown man, he once willingly submitted himself to a hypnotist, but turned out to be a poor subject, unable to go under. He could not relinquish power to another. (Is this why his poems fail to be moving? The "frenzy," the "abandon," the "madness" of the poet are not in him.) (I should note here that of all his published work, according to his own statement, only his poems now "embarrass" him.)

Perhaps most revealing on this same theme is his attitude toward money. A friend once suggested to him that he buy a car: "This shocked me. I had never thought of myself as a possible car owner. Nor had it occurred to me that money was something that could be spent. Automatically I always had hoarded it, spending as little as possible."

On the other hand, there are one or two moments that are lyrical and lovely (although he offers not nearly as much of these as in the fiction). His first view of North Africa is moving: "On the second day at dawn I went on deck and saw the rugged line of the mountains of Algeria ahead. . . . Like any Romantic, I had always been vaguely certain that sometime during my life I should come into a magic place which in disclosing its secrets would give me wisdom and ecstasy— perhaps even death. And now, as I stood in the wind looking at the mountains ahead, I felt the stirring of the engine within, and it was as if I were drawing close to the solution of an as-yet-unposed problem. I was incredibly happy as I watched the wall of mountains slowly take on substance, but I let the happiness wash over me and asked no questions."

Some years later, asleep one night in New York, he had a dream: "This dream was distinctive because although short and with no anecdotal content beyond that of a changing succession of streets, after I awoke, it had left its essence with me in a state of enameled precision: a residue of ineffable sweetness and calm. In the late afternoon sunlight I walked slowly through complex and tunneled streets. As I reviewed it, lying there, sorry to have left the place behind, I realized with a jolt that the magic city really existed. It was Tangier. My heart accelerated, and memories of other courtyards and stairways flooded in, still fresh from sixteen years before."

Later that same day, riding the Fifth Avenue bus, he suddenly discovered within him the title, main characters and plot outline of his first and glorious novel, *The Sheltering Sky*.

On balance, though, this book and the life it represents are peculiarly flat.

He seems to admit this, on the very last page, a summing-up: "In my tale . . . there are no dramatic victories because there was no struggle. I hung on and waited."

*

The career of Paul Bowles seems to parallel that of more than one American novelist: an early, brilliant, original work that fails to become the foundation for future building. Hubert Selby, Jr. (*Last Exit to Brooklyn*), Douglas Woolf (*Fade Out*), and Wright Morris (the early novels) come to mind. At times, even the reading public seems to respond in this way or expects this to happen: Herman Melville made a big splash with his first novel *Typee*, while his mature work, *Moby-Dick*, was not recognized as such.

Is this something in the American character, that we are so good at "fresh starts," not so good at sustaining? It's tempting to think of it this way, and to think of it as a legacy of the frontier—that there is always a place in which a fresh start may be made. If you mess up in Massachusetts, there's always California. And beyond California, Alaska . . .

America, at times, seems to be the only country to have gone directly from adolescence to senility, without intervention. That thought, I imagine, expresses a pessimism with which Mr. Bowles would be entirely at home.

1982

17

Carl O. Sauer

Northern Mists. By Carl O. Sauer.

At any given time in our history, there is a key word that seems to dominate the headlines. Not too long ago, it was *communist.* More recently, *ecology.* Now, suddenly, the magic word, the push-button word, is *energy.* Tiresome as it is to be assaulted daily in this way— language turned into a blunt instrument—it is made no less disturbing by the realization of the crisis the word represents: gluttonous abuse of the world's natural resources.

As Americans of some degree of consciousness, we tend to feel guilty about this, or alienated from our fellow citizens, as though gluttony and abuse of resources were a peculiarly American invention. Certainly our history has provided peculiar and spectacular expression for this force, but, as Sauer points out, this country would never have been discovered and developed had it not been for gluttonous abuse of resources by our forebears in the classical world of the Mediterranean.

Northern Mists deals primarily with seafaring and exploration in the North Atlantic, but Sauer is not satisfied to enter his subject before digging out some of the motivations, exploring in areas beyond what he so accurately calls "the limited preoccupations of political history." Back, then, to the Mediterranean, mare nostrum of the Greeks and Romans, and of the Middle Ages. He points out that the inland sea provided a relatively low yield of seafood, that the lands around it have been "plowed overlong, to grow wheat and barley, over-grazed, and depleted of trees. The whole length of the Mediterranean is scarred by man's wastage of the soil, here by gullies, there by the mineral color of subsoil from which the topsoil has been stripped."

Sounds familiar, doesn't it? But at that time, civilized man had somewhere else to go, and it was the search for pelagic protein— whales and fish—that led him to the North Atlantic coast.

Here, now, with the stage set, Sauer lays out his territory: the

North Atlantic—isolating it from the balance of the ocean as a natural region, whose cold waters produce abundance of plankton and fish: "It has been estimated that the English Channel produces annually thirteen tons of organic matter per hectare, which is about twice the yield of a good meadow in a good year in those parts."

The book proceeds, deploying the various European peoples into these waters. The Portuguese discovered the Azores and used them as a convenient midway point, from Lisbon to the codbanks off Newfoundland. The sailing ships from Bristol, England, were aware of the codbanks and the land beyond them well before Columbus. They spoke of voyages of discovery, but why did they load so much salt if not to cure fish? The Basques, on the Bay of Biscay, practiced their own abuse of a resource, the right whale being overfished and destroyed in that area, the Basques being forced out to sea to replenish. The Norse settlers of Greenland used to trap polar-bear cubs and ship them to Europe, one of them finding its way to the Sultan of Egypt (what an image!—the Sultan and his polar bear, floating down the Nile). The Irish were perhaps guided by migrating swans to the discovery of Iceland, a hundred years before the Norsemen arrived. And Sauer makes a strong case for Irish missionary settlements in the Western Hemisphere before the arrival of the Vikings. The newly discovered "Viking" village, at L'Anse aux Meadows, Newfoundland, would seem to be Irish rather than Norse.

Sauer's surfaces are as interesting as his depths. He loves the language, gently, without exploitation, and the deliberate flow of words is a delight. Speaking of herring, he says, "At the time of the spawning runs they are mature, gravid with roe and milt, in prime condition." For a chapter heading, there is the phrase, "Dark Ages and Tenebrous Sea." He speaks repeatedly of that auspicious Viking lady, Aud the Deep-Minded. And at times the language becomes so lyrical that it is possible to compose a poem from it.

Fundamentally, however, it is his depths that hold us, offered without pretension, but simply, deliberately, in a language that works for him.

1974

18

The Making of a Play

In February, 1979, I was introduced to John Dillon and Sara O'Conner, artistic director and managing director, respectively, of the Milwaukee Repertory Theater. This was arranged by the indefatigable Karl Gartung, manager of that remarkable Milwaukee bookstore, Woodland Pattern.

John and Sara had been reading some of my books, and we listened to a tape of a reading I had given. They asked me if I would be interested in putting together a play made up of materials from various of my books, and would I then come to Milwaukee to direct it.

I had a year to think about this while plans were made, funds were raised, etc. Although I had done some work in theater, both as actor and playwright, thirty-five years ago, I had broken with theater—under the influence more of poets and novelists—with strong feelings about the impurity of theater as a medium, feelings that sustained the separation during those thirty-five years.

It was curious, therefore, to have professional theater people—John and Sara—looking into my work, finding something I felt I had abjured. And this led me to examine again my thoughts about theater, to discover what theater is, for me; to determine if I still find it an impure medium . . . or is there such a thing as "pure" theater?

I was flattered, challenged, and a little nervous, I guess, in consideration of the great liberty John and Sara had given me—to write as I please; and the responsibility—to serve as both playwright and director, working with experienced professional actors. It was clear that the enterprise was developed largely for the benefit of the actors, as an exercise for them, an engagement with language and mime outside their usual range.

I was told there would be four actors; the play should be written with this number in mind. Initially, I didn't know whether they would be male, female, or a mix; in fact, the play was written and finished with the consideration that I might have men playing women, or vice versa, or blacks playing whites, etc., and that this would be simply another challenge to the actor or actress, another "illusion" to be dealt with.

Getting down to the work of writing, I went through all my books and unpublished manuscripts, looking for episodes, chapters, vignettes that suggested *movement*, where I found myself visualizing live bodies behind or amidst the language. This did not necessarily involve dialogue; in fact, as it turned out, there was very little dialogue, so that when it did occur, it came, I felt, with a certain freshness. Instead, there was a good deal of action, or mime, described either by the participants or by narrators.

I came up with a surprising number of possible scenes, some of them highly complex. My original version, I suddenly realized, would run some three-and-a-half hours—I had to whittle it down to an hour and a half. I finally got it into two acts and sixteen scenes, and it began to take a certain obvious shape and form: it became apparent that I was putting together a kind of American history and that the scenes should be placed in chronological order, running from the Cherokee myths (that I had taken from *Will West*), through Columbus (from *Genoa*), to the Civil War (from *Waters of Potowmack*). I called it *An American Chronicle*.

From the beginning, the idea was *simplicity*. Well after I had planned and written the play, I read Jerzy Grotowski ("Towards a Poor Theater") and felt my notions confirmed . . . that the centripetal force of theater drives toward the actor; that the actor is voice and body; that theater, therefore, in its simplest terms, is language and mime.

The language exists already in the text. And the play should be a joy and satisfaction to read, by itself, *before* it is embodied on the stage . . . so that the act of giving the words to actors, adding flesh, limbs and movement to language, is an enrichment of forces already present.

Grotowski pleads that it is absurd for theater to compete with film and television in the realm of costume, setting, props, lights, special effects, transitions, etc. Just as representational painting became somewhat absurd with the development of the camera, so representational theater became somewhat of an anachronism.

The set for *An American Chronicle* was to be simply a platform. Later this was elaborated to two platforms, and masked entrances upstage. Costumes for the four actors were uniform: blue jeans, T-shirts and sneakers. Lighting was of the simplest, and the actors could be seen moving between scenes and seated offstage. Props consisted of a tambourine, for one scene. Sound effects: a harmonica (one scene), and an actor beating his hands on a wooden cube to simulate gunfire (one scene). Scripts were carried in hand for some of the scenes, others were memorized; in some cases, the scripts were integrated into the substance of the play. (One audience member told me that the play should never be memorized, that the scripts were a positive *addition*.)

Because of this simplicity, transitions from scene to scene were executed rapidly, and contrasts from scene to scene—in pace, tone, substance—were enjoyed in a way that a cumbersome production never would have allowed.

As it turned out, I had four male actors, all white, ranging in age from early twenties to late thirties. As I look back now, I would say that one of the four was absolutely brilliant; two were above average; and one was competent, but with a large and volatile ego.

The most difficult part of directing came on the first day: I had to meet the actors, none of whom I had seen before; try to give them some sense of what the play was about, what I was attempting; and cast the play at once, all sixteen scenes, before rehearsals could begin.

I became aware of a peculiar double dynamic at work in my relation to the actors. On one level, I was their superior: the playwright, the director, the "literary" man, a good deal older than they—someone in whom John and Sara obviously believed, or I wouldn't have been there. On another level, that of experience in theater, I was at best a neophyte, and possibly an ignoramus. This became touchy at times, particularly in my dealings with the scene-stealing propensities of the man with the volatile ego.

All the actors, however, without exception, were cooperative, trying to deal sincerely with these factors.

The casting, of course, was crucial, and here I was either shrewd or lucky: as I came to know the actors, their limits and abilities, during later rehearsals, I don't think I would have changed a single casting decision that I had made on the first day. For example, I had a scene taken from Walt Whitman, his account of the defeated Union soldiers straggling into Washington after first Battle of Manassas: the man I cast as Whitman told me, *after* I had cast him, that he had done a one-man Whitman show ... his knowledge of Whitman far exceeded mine, and he brought this to bear on the role in several useful ways.

91

In another case, the man I cast as John Wilkes Booth, mouthing materials taken from his diary, had great difficulty with the role; I asked him to ham it up, emote all over the place, break all the rules of good acting, let it all hang out, etc.—and he was oddly stymied. This was the closest I came to changing a casting, in midrehearsal. I let him struggle, however, and quite on his own he came up with a marvelous device: to break the monologue into sections, play each part of it as a different Shakesperian villain—Iago, Richard III, etc.

The actors were professionals, Equity members, with years of experience. But none of them had been trained in mime. And none of them, I think, had done anything quite like this before. The play at times called for silent mime, it called for speakers describing an action mimed, it called for actors miming and speaking at once, it called for conventional dialogue, it called for language with little or no mime. After rehearsals were over and we were in production, the actors became candid with me about the difficulties. One spoke of the difficulty in communication, the fact that they and I didn't share a common language. Another spoke of a particular scene, "John Marr," a long quote from Melville with very little stage action: how he hated that scene at the beginning, couldn't understand or mouth the language, how he came around to it, learned to love the language, it became one of his favorite scenes.

Three of the actors bought several of the books from which the play was drawn.

Response of the actors and audience demonstrated a point of which I think I was aware from the start: *An American Chronicle* steers a narrow course between literature and theater, drawing on resources of both. One of the actors said that, in the process of rehearsal, "we simplified." I think he meant by this the process of translating or transposing language into bodily action, and it is interesting to me that a theater person would think of that as "simplifying."

My effort in all the books, beginning with *Will West*, has been to collapse time, to create a plane on which events of all periods may occur at once, to create tensions that one finds in the static arts, that I found so forceful, for example, in the color associations of Josef Albers—the chemistry of a red against a green, etc. Can these tensions be created in theater? To read a book requires *time*, although a reader is somewhat in control of that time, being able to go backward, forward, etc. Watching a play or hearing a symphony, the audience is locked into the time sequence. There is no "going back," save in memory.

An American Chronicle, as the title suggests, is a chronology, a sequence. Before writing the script, I read Aeschylus, listened to Bach, Ives, Coltrane and Mingus. At some point, I realized that Ives and the jazz composers were not appropriate, or could not be factored into this effort. But *An American Chronicle* is a first: for myself as playwright, for myself as director, and for the actors, in this kind of theater. It is interesting to me that the three performances of the play represented a progression, each successively better than the one before, as the actors became more comfortable with the material.

I'm not at all sure that the complexities of Ives and Mingus, a complexity in which events occur on a single plane and all the lines are tense or taut—I'm not at all sure that this isn't possible in theater. And this idea represents a challenge.

N.d.

19

Totem Paul: A Self-Review

The other day, my three-and-a-half-year-old granddaughter Rachel saw a totem pole, and she wanted to know all about it, who carved it, why there was a bird at the top, etc. So the next day I went to the children's room at the local library and said to the lady in charge, "totem poles."

She came forth with one of those marvelous books that one occasionally finds, written for children. Direct, factual, straightforward—don't try to bullshit a kid!—the book laid out in good, clean prose, and in just a few pages, everything one would want to know as an introduction to totem poles: what they are, what they mean, who made them, where and when, how they were made, what is being done now to save them, etc.

Rachel and I looked at the pictures, and then she quickly lost interest. But not grandpapa. I brought the book home and read it carefully.

*

A totem pole was in no sense a religious icon or object; the Indian did not think of it as representing his spiritual life. Commissioned by a wealthy chief and carved by a team of expert craftsmen, it was an historical record, from animal to man, of the clan or tribe to which the chief belonged. Neither patron nor craftsman was aiming for spiritual or aesthetic qualities; the intent, rather, was for historical accuracy. And it is for this very reason—because they were not trying consciously to be beautiful—that so many of the totem poles are, in fact, so extraordinarily beautiful. It is the virtue of indirection.

Studying a complex totem pole, one can see how the various figures, and the tales they represent, bear upon one another: the claws of the raven are on the back of the beaver, etc. I realized that I

94

was dealing here with an unusual hybrid form: generally, works of art fall into one of two categories, those that may be taken in at once, like a painting or a sculpture, and those that require time for their reception, such as a symphony, a play or a book. A totem pole combines both conditions: one can see it at a glance, or one can read it like a book, the chapters merging, top to bottom, or bottom to top. And to describe this mix, I have come up with the term, "The Narrative Hieroglyph."

*

Genoa is the last book I wrote which may be described as a novel. Guy Davenport calls it an architectonic novel. Since then, with the fiction dropped out, I think all of my books, individually and collectively, may be called "narrative hieroglyphs." True, unlike a totem pole, a book may not be taken in at a glance; it requires time to read. But a totem pole, as I have said, may be read like a book. And the effect of one of my books—which I have commissioned myself to carve, to record the "histories" of our "tribes"—the effect is one of the various elements or "figures," in a line sequence, each perched upon the back of its predecessor. In the past I have used terms such as "mosaic" or "collage"; but the totem pole, with its tribal, historic sequence and organic juxtapositions, is a much more powerful analog.

*

One final point. I know of a poet today who writes his poems on expensive acid-free paper designed to last forever. He is consciously and directly courting posterity.

But posterity, like beauty, is unpredictable and responds best to indirection. The Indian chief who commissioned a totem pole intended it to last only his lifetime . . . let his heirs and successors make their own. In fact, due to exposure to weather, many of the finest poles have fallen, rotted and disappeared. It is the archival white man, with his hunger for aesthetics, who is now preserving them, bringing them indoors, oiling and staining them.

The Indians who made them were concerned only with the making of the object in the moment, the object finished and raised. Let the future take care of itself. It is perhaps the intensity of the moment, carved into the figures, that gives the poles the very posterity of which the chief and his artisans were heedless.

*

Am I courting posterity with my books? Well, not consciously. How could I care, or what good will it do me, what people think of the books after I'm gone? I would like to see them read *now*. They are printed on what paper the publisher chooses, to last as long as it may . . . the books to be reprinted as anyone may or may not wish, as time goes on.

Let the future take care of itself.

N.d.

20

Olympian Impressions

There are areas on the surface of the earth where the landscape or, often, the conjunction of landscape and climate are so dramatic, not to say melodramatic, as to be the primary and unrelenting daily challenge to one's attentions. The north shore of the Olympic Peninsula, where I am now visiting, strikes me as such a place.

The sky is seldom altogether clear; more often there is cloud cover; or, more often still, a shifting—and quickly shifting—succession of clouds, of sunlight dimmed through shallow clouds, of narrow shafts of sunlight patching the water surface. As Nancy says, it looks like pewter.

Our house overlooks Admiralty Inlet, at the junction of the Strait of Juan de Fuca—opening, as we know, to the ocean, far to the west—and Puget Sound—with Seattle, Tacoma and Bremerton to the east. When the sun *does* shine, we have clear views of pine bluffs, beach and water; of Indian, Marrowstone and Whidbey Islands; in the distance, Mount Rainier, in the center of the view; to the left, the Northern Cascades, with Mt. Baker permanently snowcapped; and to the right, the jagged Olympics.

This is what we see through the sliding glass doors in the dining area or through the window over the sink in the kitchen. It is what commands our attention many, many times each day—from our first arising in the morning to the last light at nightfall.

We are living on the outskirts of Port Townsend, a relict Victorian village that boomed and busted along about 1890 and that still retains much architectural charm, although being nibbled, now, by strip development at the edges. Because of this charm, because, by West-Coast standards, it is "old," Port Townsend is now expensive and chic. Boutiques, antiques, bed-and-breakfast mansions, etc.; well-heeled Wisconsin retirees; Californians weary of their hot tubs, now looking for something "real"; trust-fund hippies, off the slopes at Aspen; day-trippers from Seattle; young survivors, scratching a living at the edges, etc.

Along with all this, of course, Port Townsend has become "artsy";

there are painting, poetry, crafts. And what little I have seen of this so far presents an odd appearance: if the artists were attracted, presumably by landscape and climate, they are producing work that is strangely disconnected from just those factors; it could be anywhere—Provincetown, Soho, the Berkshires—or Port Townsend.

There is one exception that I have discovered so far, a man named C., who lives, appropriately enough and by choice, not in Port Townsend but in ugly, roughneck, redneck Port Angeles, a nearby lumber and fishing town. C. has been meeting the challenge head-on, exploring and painting the shoreline, foothills and mountains, the cloud and landshapes, with wonderful persistence, for years. I have seen examples of his work in dated sequence, and one can follow the growing intensity, the meticulousness, the forces channeled.

I am also aware that C. has been married and divorced twice, and that no human figures, or even human artifacts, appear in his recent paintings. The specifics of what the landscape offers him command his constant, almost ferocious attention: a concentration of energy that works well in the paintings but that might not be easy to accommodate in a human relationship.

Is this what the landscape does to one?

*

Shortly after arriving, we drove from Port Townsend to Port Angeles along Routes 20 and 101, the latter the highway that makes the circuit of the Peninsula. Initially a pretty road, somewhat hilly, through evergreen forests, with occasional glimpses of water, it takes us first to Discovery Bay, known to the locals as Disco Bay—the village itself a grungy little roadside excrescence. It is a curiosity of the times that the two most famous representatives of Olympic cuisine—Dungeness crab and the native oyster—are not to be found in the markets of Port Townsend. For these one drives twelve miles, to a run-down general store in Disco Bay. And the crabs are all precooked, the oysters shucked and jarred.

Next, driving westward, there is Gardiner, whose general store contains what has got to be the dirtiest, most dilapidated branch of the United States Postal Service to be found on the face of this our fair land. I have no confidence that the letter I mailed there ever went beyond the bottom of the dusty slot where I dropped it.

Beyond Gardiner is Blyn, and on to Sequim—pronounced *Skwim*. From Blyn to Sequim. Whereas Disco Bay and Gardiner were simply old and grungy, Sequim is modern and affluent, and the strip development, both in and out of town, assaults both sides of the highway like a flash flood, a slap in the face.

From Sequim to Port Angeles the highway is pockmarked with little disasters. And Port Angeles, the "big city" of the peninsula, with fish and lumber money, is the vulgarity of Sequim compounded exponentially.

Here we pick up C. He tells us that he likes Port Angeles, that all those cancers along the highway help to preserve the landscape; they keep the white trash, and many of the tourists, huddled to the asphalt. In five or ten minutes off 101, one can be in time immemorial.

With C. as guide, we drive into the Olympics. First the foothills, on the very edge of Port Angeles: rolling, open farmland, with a backdrop of jagged mountains. For the first time here—and perhaps for the first time in my life—I have a genuine feel for the word "homestead." Despite the occasional jeep or chain saw, it is frontier, pure nineteenth century.

We drive further into the mountains, to some old, man-made lakes that antedate the establishment of the national park. The dams have been condemned by the Corps of Engineers, but nobody much cares; should they go, only the Indian reservation below would be wiped out.

On to Crescent Lake, and here we park the car and hike into what is my sense of the rain forest—although I'm told the true rain forest is further west, where the rainfall is 150 inches annually. Nevertheless, here we have enormous firs and hemlock, moss all over everything; and the nursing trees, trees that fall and serve as sustenance for new sprouts, which then grow and become enormous.

We are following a mountain stream—the water a curious gray, or (again) pewter color—and come, at the head of our hike, to a powerful waterfall: volumes of water forced into a long, narrow drop. Everything here is cool, wet, gray, potent and channeled.

Lunch this day is taken at a roadside café, where we have "widow-makers," with "timber logs." These turn out to be hamburgers on sourdough toast, and french fries with the skins on.

Driving is a challenge, with the huge lumber trucks menacing us at every curve.

99

Quite a day.

*

Indian Island, directly in the view from our cottage, is taken over largely by the U.S. Navy. Mile after mile of immaculate chain-link fence, with signs, "Government Property. KEEP OUT." I'm told that every incoming vessel carrying live ammo is required to stop here and unload before entering Puget Sound. And I am told of a local girl, just out of high school, who was hired by the Navy—at minimum wage—to count the bombs. She finally couldn't stand it, quit her job, went to work at the local health food store.

*

Port Townsend is ringed by three abandoned army bases, now state parks, all with massive, rotting gun emplacements. These were constructed at enormous expense during the Spanish-American War to defend the entrance to the sound against an utterly non-existent enemy fleet. Today they are beautiful.

*

When one arrives in a new community, a roadside café, preferably an older one—as William Least Heat Moon has pointed out—is a likely place to get a feel for the area; or, at least, a look at the faces that inhabit it. Another likely spot is the public library; the types—the retirees, the cranks, the eccentrics, the family historians—who spend their days reading the papers, snoozing, gossiping, perhaps mulling over some real or invented research project. Again, the faces.

I drove out again one day, stopping in a coffee shop in Sequim, observing the country types, the farmers, the ranchers, and then went on to Port Angeles, where I spent the day in research at the library. It struck me that, among the men at least, I was seeing the same face, or a varying version of it, over and over again. And it was a face, or a look at least, that I had seen before: on C., and on another friend T., who was raised in nearby Bremerton.

Years ago I went to an exhibition of Rembrandt paintings, portrait after portrait of the aged, the faces heavily lined, incised like a relief map, each line seeming to mark an episode or an epoch in the subject's life, so that the face became an autobiography, and one felt that imminent death would be a natural conclusion, the completion of a life fully lived and recorded.

These peninsula faces, however—and I'm speaking now of the older ones—are altogether different. However old they are, there seems to be an underlying freshness, a bloom of youth, across which age, as an instant event rather than process, has been suddenly slapped, like a flash flood. So that the face is not a map, not an autobiography, because the young man, who has barely learned how to live, let alone record his life, is still in there, peering out through clear-blue, somewhat watery eyes, with a look that is plainly abashed over what has happened to him. Again and again I have seen this same face, this same look.

A friend who has lived in coastal areas of England, as well as here, points out the similarities in climate, and says that the high degree of moisture in the air, the frequent rains, may be responsible for the fresh complexions to be found in both areas. I wonder. This may well be part of it; yet I believe that I've been observing a genuine peninsula type, perhaps Northwest type, because it goes beyond mere complexion, it is often a shape of face, or, more importantly, a look in the eye, that denotes a shared character. It isn't even furtive, because it hasn't had that much time to think about itself. It is a quiet shock of surprise: what has happened to me?

*

I return now to the four general areas discovered thus far: 1) artsy, self-conscious Port Townsend; 2) some lovely, backwater, home-steading farmland; 3) the unspeakable trash of Route 101, Sequim and Port Angeles; and 4) the pure wilderness, the Olympics.

I'm told that 80% of the peninsula is in national park or forest. A look at the map would seem to confirm this. The wilderness will be preserved.

Port Townsend will probably thrive, becoming less and less what it pretends to be the more it succeeds. But it remains an isolated pocket.

The homesteaders, the less affluent retirees or survivors who are seeking a quiet life, will probably retain pockets of attractive farm-land—land that for one reason or another nobody else wants.

Most of what happens on the peninsula, though, is tied up with communities such as Sequim and Port Angeles, and stripped along 101. I can't help feeling that the unspeakable chrome and plastic vulgarity, the planned obsolescence of these communities, slapped across the face of the land—leaving the land looking somewhat abashed—is more than just a metaphor for what I take to be the characteristic Olympic face: the little boy peering out, too surprised to be hurt, from behind the hard fact of age, an age that has only just this moment been slapped upon him.

1983

21

The Business of Poetry

"The United States is the world's first nation to go directly from adolescence to senility, without the intervention of maturity." That is a truism—or witticism—or both—that has been kicking around in my head for many years. I don't know whether I invented it or stole it. No matter. It is probably not original.

I think it has something to do, much to do, with the question at hand—the business of poetry; with the aborted growth of so many poets, the subtle diversion from original aspirations.

*

Any young American who charts a course wherein the financial rewards are not clearly in sight necessarily leads a strange and uncomfortable life. While adhering to the principles that dictated the choice, one is constantly vulnerable to two nagging seductions: first, money, and all that it can bring; and secondly, fame.

In free-enterprise capitalism, with greed sanctified, the lure of money is always with us. But fame, I think, as an expectation, is peculiar to only two professions in America: sports and the arts. (Perhaps also politics, where it is impossible to succeed without being known.) The gifted athlete or the rock star can expect fame and expect it fast. To a lesser extent, so can the poet. At least, he has the example of those whose names are known in literate circles, whose books are read and taught across the land, and who, in consequence, command the better teaching jobs and reading fees. As I have pointed out, except for politics and sports, this expectation of fame is peculiar to the arts. How many lawyers, doctors, electricians, plumbers, and architects enter their professions or trades *expecting* to become famous?

There is a special affinity, I think, between the poet and the rock musician—particularly when the poet goes on the reading circuit, becomes a performing artist. There was tacit recognition of this when Allen Ginsberg and Bob Dylan went on tour together. They share a nominal common currency in language, although this is minimal in most rock music. And they also share in music, to the extent that all language is musical. But more to the point, the poet has before him, constantly, the example of the rock musician who becomes rich and famous at a very early age.

Beginning, I suppose, with Hollywood, but affected more by the great dislocations caused by World Wars I and II, and now the computer revolution, time sense in America has become grossly skewed. Most young writers I know live in terror of those great watersheds, the birthdays marking the decades in their lives: ages twenty, thirty, and forty. Forty, I think, is the crucial one: beyond this, it is no longer useful to be "promising"; by now, there must be solid accomplishment and consequent recognition, or it all goes down the drain.

This is a novel phenomenon, novel to the present generation. I have great difficulty explaining to young students how it could be that Herman Melville wrote *Moby-Dick* when he was thirty-two, that it was badly received, that he lived and wrote for more than forty years longer, that he died in obscurity, and that he remained obscure for more than thirty years after his death.

(The one person whose recognition Melville most actively sought was Hawthorne, and Hawthorne evidently responded enthusiastically to *Moby-Dick*. In thanks, Melville wrote to him as follows: "People think that if a man has undergone any hardship, he should have a reward; but for my part, if I have done the hardest possible day's work, and then come to sit down in a corner & eat my supper comfortably—why, then I don't think I deserve any reward for my hard day's work—for am I not now at peace? Is not my supper good? My peace and my supper are my reward, my dear Hawthorne. So your joy-giving and exultation-breeding letter is not my reward for my ditcher's work with that book, but is the good goddess's bonus over and above what was stipulated for—for not one man in five cycles, who is wise, will expect appreciative recognition from his fellows, or any one of them. Appreciation! Recognition! Is love appreciated? Why, ever since Adam, who has got to the meaning of this great allegory—the world? Then we pygmies must be content to have our paper allegories but ill comprehended.")

The kind of patience required of Melville—postmortem patience, no less!—is simply baffling to most young writers today. I have had students, age seventeen, come to me and ask how they go about having their poems copyrighted. Paranoid before they start! If they are serious, they push forward, past age twenty, past thirty, approaching forty—and here the terrors set in. Generally speaking, the subtle shifts towards careerism become evident: how can I get published here? who is sleeping with whom? if I praise her, will she praise me? whom should I stroke to get invited to teach at the writers' conference? etc.

And all this occurs just at the entrance upon what are, in the normal course of things, the mature middle years, when human capabilities are at their richest and ripest.

Hence, the truism: Americans pass, sadly enough, often enough, from adolescence to senility, without mature intervention.

*

One could legislate the MFA writing courses, the NEA grants, etc., out of existence, returning to some sort of Darwinian state, where only the toughest and truest (and independently wealthy) survive. But it's not going to happen. The students, the poets, the teachers all demand these services. No bureaucracy once established ever dismantles itself. I think it was Guy Davenport who said that literature used to be a river running between banks, now it's a river running through an ocean. The winnowing process that took so long in Melville's case is now infinitely more crowded and complex; but it will still happen.

Meanwhile, a number of poets, both good and bad, some with academic degrees, some without, are enabled to teach these courses. The jobs offer a wage, and, depending on one's energies and temperament, this may or may not be better than driving a taxi or tending bar. And although the students may not be greatly helped, they're probably not badly harmed.

And no doubt each generation of this literary river, coursing through the great ocean of scribblers, will yield up roughly the same number of genuine poets as before: the few who somehow or other buck the prevailing current and make their way to some extended growth and ripening.

1983

105

22

The Creative Process

Choice of the daunting title for this essay is deliberate. In opening a magazine, we all tend to skim titles and authors' names to determine which pieces we want to read, and I am fully aware that this title will cause many a reader to skip on by or at least begin reading with an unconscious negative bias.

There is good reason for this. Experience teaches us that whenever an editor invites a so-called "creative" person to diagnose and expatiate on the so-called "creative" process within that holy instrument that is his or her own "creative" self, said editor is opening the floodgates to a seemingly endless freshet of mystical nonsense.

The fact is, few of us who write or paint or compose or otherwise "create" know what the hell it is we're doing. In general, if we're any good at what we do, we're moving too fast, too much in thrall to our obsession, our muse, our daemon, to be intelligently aware of process.

But that ignorance doesn't seem to stop us. Given permission by a well-meaning editor, we're off to the races. And it piles up. And piles up. And piles up.

Very well. Don't say that you haven't been warned. *Caveat lector!*

*

I have always been fascinated by the term *the quick and the dead*, as though there were no allowance for anything in between. One cannot be slow or lethargic or lazy. One is quick. Or one is dead.

The confusion, of course, derives from earlier meanings of the word *quick*. It meant, originally, to be alive. An entity that is quickened is given life. *Quick* is associated with *quiver*, *quaver*, and

106

quake—all very early signs of vitality.

Another synonym for *quick* is *sprightly*, and this leads us into the manifold layers of meanings deriving from the Latin *spirare*, to breathe.

Latin offers two words meaning to breathe—*halare* and *spirare*—but *halare* seems to describe merely the mechanical process, whereas *spirare* brings us to the noun *spiritus*, whose meanings unfold from breathing and breath to include air, life, soul, pride and courage. In English we may be spiritual, spirited, sprightly, and in good spirits; we may indulge in ardent spirits, and may be spirited away to the spirit world.

There is little we can do without breath, without spirit. We aspire, conspire and perspire. All that transpires requires respiration. In sadness we suspire, and eventually we expire. But—and here we come around at length to the topic of our discussion—we may, at one or more points in our lives, if we are creative souls—we may become *inspired!*

*

Inspiration.

The intake of breath.

The way that something exceptionally beautiful—or exceptionally frightening—causes one, *involuntarily*, "to catch one's breath."

Is this what true poetic inspiration is?

*

I find myself now standing on the tip end of the diving board, my knees quivering, quavering and quaking, as I'm about to take the plunge into a great bath of mystical nonsense.

I step back, try to feel solid ground under me.

I remind myself that I've always been suspicious of people who claim William Blake as a cultural ancestor. The watery, distant look in the eyes, the tendency to talk about "the infinite," "the light," "paradise," etc., to indicate that they have already taken the plunge

107

from which I have just stepped back.

Is there such a thing as too much inspiration? Too much breath?

To compound my metaphors: it is not a good idea to catch one's breath when one is under water.

*

If not mystical inspiration—then what are we talking about?

A couple of quotations might be useful here. Edgar Allan Poe: "There is no greater mistake than the supposition that a true originality is a mere matter of impulse or inspiration. To originate is carefully, patiently, and understandingly to combine."

Herman Melville: "And here it may be randomly suggested . . . whether some things men think they do not know, are not for all that thoroughly comprehended by them; and yet, so to speak, though contained in themselves, are kept a secret from themselves."

The Poe remark is perhaps oversimplified, but is valuable, at least as a corrective.

Melville's thought is more complex, involving areas of experience, of conscious/unconscious knowledge and data, that we know or do not know or do not think we know that is factored in some physiological way into our being, and that may be a larger element than we are aware of than that which flies under the airy banner of "inspiration."

Julian Jaynes, in *The Origin of Consciousness in the Breakdown of the Bicameral Mind,* claims that early, preconscious man lived his life largely by habit, and whenever he found himself in a situation requiring a decision, the right lobe of the brain gave orders to the left, and the left promptly executed them. These were auditory hallucinations: preconscious man heard voices, and he projected them into an elaborate structure that he called "the gods." As the cities grew larger, life became more complex and sophisticated, and modern consciousness came into being, the voices of the gods became weaker and more confused; no longer did they speak forth, clear and true, in any place and at any time . . . their appearances became ritualized and isolated, and, most particularly, they could be expected to

108

perform in only a few unique and geographically dramatic places.

This period of overlap—between the primitive and the sophisticated, preconscious and conscious—began some three-thousand years ago, and, according to Jaynes, it is still going on. As the gods retreated, became increasingly temperamental, it was the oracles and the poets who became increasingly important: the former, as the channel through whom the gods occasionally spoke, and the latter, the poets, as the ones especially sensitive to the gods' places, and as the gatherers, presenters and at times performers of a people's history, the restructuring of the preconscious era, that time of infallible authorization, for which modern man, capable and confused, has never lost his nostalgia.

Following left-lobe-right-lobe theory, the gods speak to us from the right lobe, the intuitive lobe. In the case of Joan of Arc, the voices of her saints spoke to her, literally, in her garden. Such voices, in Melville's words, are "things men think they do not know" but "are not for all that thoroughly comprehended by them; and yet, so to speak, though contained in themselves, are kept a secret from themselves."

We are inspired, take in a breath; and when we die, we expire, and are spirited off to the spirit world.

But here again I approach the diving board, knees quivering . . . and again I step back. Back to crazy Edgar Poe. Because it is not just inspiration, not the involuntary intake of breath—it is knowledge, the fruit of hard experience, things we do and do not know, brought to the surface.

Brought up carefully, patiently . . . but at times, also, *quickly!*

*

David Kadlec, in an unpublished essay, describes the theory of *bricolage*, as developed by the French anthropologist, Claude Lévi-Strauss: "*Bricolage* is distinguished from the work of the craftsman insofar as the materials used are those salvaged from the wreckage of previous constructions rather than materials designed specifically for the task at hand. Lévi-Strauss views mythical thought, which draws from an extensive but limited repertoire, as a kind of intellectual *bricolage.* New myths can be wrought exclusively from the fragments of old ones."

Fragments of old myths, old voices, are caught up as they float to the surface. Original meanings may be lost or incomprehensible or conceived only in the abstract. But carefully and patiently put together in new relationships and in a current context, they are charged with new force.

In our multiethnic, multicultural, severely disjointed world, *bricolage* may be our most natural mode.

*

It is sometimes forgotten that a work of art is conceived and brought to life by a process of *in*direction. We are all familiar with the metaphor of courting the muse. Courting—or, more bluntly, seducing—the muse involves all manner of guile and ruse. I remember reading a poem some years back in which the poet speaks directly, bitterly, to the muse: "You squint when you read my poems!" This may relieve the poet's feelings, but it won't impress the muse. I don't think she likes to be addressed directly. And it is plainly obvious that she doesn't want to be raped. Going back to etymology, *to seduce* means *to lead aside.* This implies that the muse has another purpose from which the successful poet is able to divert her, distract her. There are indications that, when circumstances are just right, the muse enjoys playing this game, this dance of courtship and seduction—both for the pleasures of the process and for its ultimate intention and culmination. But, given the cultural explosion in this country today, the proliferation of little mags, etc., she would appear to have more suitors than Penelope. And I suspect she is particularly resistant to those with the boldest and least subtle blandishments.

Bearing all this in mind, I am amazed at the number of poets and other artists in America today who are throwing themselves upon the muse in full frontal attack. Each has made a "commitment to Art," or a "commitment to a Life in Art." All other human, social, ethical bridges have been burned; the poet is out there naked and alone before the muse . . . and he or she seems to behave as though the muse were exclusively attentive.

It is my feeling that this direct approach is often self-defeating.

110

These are the artists who seem the least self-critical, the least aware of both the virtues and vices of their own work. Encapsulated in their fundamental commitment, they have denied themselves all manner of leverage. Often they wind up simply playing a role, fulfilling an image: "I, the artist" or "I, the poet."

Most parents are surprised, be it positively or negatively, by the choices their children make for lifetime partners. For those of us who follow the arts, the muse similarly surprises and amazes us. Be it to the corporate executive, the family doctor, the alcoholic housemaid, or the impoverished field hand, her granting of favors seldom ceases to astonish. And she seems to take an almost perverse pleasure in passing by those who have made the most spectacular courtship displays.

*

Charles Olson once wrote, "Art is the only morality." I think this a questionable premise, on the face of it. But, more importantly, I wonder how his vision may have been damaged, how his awareness of himself and his work, particularly his later work, may have been skewed by such an absolute commitment.

On the other side of this coin, I am reminded of a book called *Landmarks of Old Prince William* by one Fairfax Harrison. Dealing with colonial Virginia, it is a work of dense scholarship written in a wonderfully open and rich prose. I was amazed, subsequently, to find out that, besides this kind of endeavor, Harrison was also president of the Southern Railway. America has produced numerous other avocational scholars like Harrison: small-town lawyers, businessmen, whatever, who kept alive aspects of their local culture. Many of them, like Harrison, wrote a remarkable prose, and I wonder how much of this ease with language stems from the fact that they were not singly committed to it; they were beneficiaries of the manifold layers of activity in their lives.

Then, of course, there were Stevens and Williams and Ives.

*

111

It is dangerous to draw absolute conclusions from the above. I could easily paint myself into a corner as isolating as that that threatens the "all-for-art" people. True creating is, at best, an obsessive, compulsive process; one accommodates it as best one can.

It is particularly dangerous to attempt conclusions that presume to apply to all historical periods. We are, so much more than we realize, the product of the history that has produced us, that has produced the culture in which we live.

It does seem to me, though, that here, today—United States, 1984—the role of "The Great Artist"—the lonely one, alone with the muse—is a romantic, nineteenth-century notion that has long outlived its value.

Perhaps the only historical constant, since man has first courted the muse, is the muse herself: a wily and wonderful and still utterly unpredictable creature.

1984

23

Preface to *Time in New England*

Time in New England. Photographs by Paul Strand;
text selected and edited by Nancy Newhall.

That the study of man is the study of migration is not a particularly
novel idea. From primitive man, wandering in search of food and in
the process peopling the world, through the historic era—the waves
of raid and conquest, crusade and retreat—man clearly has lived in
an unsettled state.

In the book *The Golden Door*, the authors point out that
migrations in the modern era have presented a somewhat different
picture:

> In certain respects the modern pattern of movement is a distinctly
> different kind of migration from the kinds that predominated in the
> centuries after the fall of Rome. The most important difference is that the
> decision to move was usually taken independently by an individual or by
> the head of a family for that family. Occasionally, small groups, such as
> the Puritan settlers of New England, moved as a group, but they were
> more the exception than the rule.

From the viewpoint of American history, this distinction between the
Puritans and other settlers is of significance. As a group or communal
movement, the Puritans alone among the major settlers submerged
individual ambition in the welfare of the community. Although the
exigencies in all the early settlements up and down the Atlantic coast
forced individuals into a kind of loose, neighborly cooperation—the
spirit of openness and friendliness that survives in the Midwest and
West today—the Puritans alone established themselves as a potent
unitary force.

They came to these shores to establish the Kingdom of Heaven on
Earth. This was no metaphor: it was a literal, overriding, single
energy governing every daily thought and act. As a corollary, and
quite beside the point in their own consciousness, they found themselves taking America seriously in a way unique among all the

113

settlers. For them, the dreadful ocean that they had crossed, separating them from England and the Church of England, was a barrier at their backs. The Southerner, by contrast, had never in his heart and mind left England. He had brought a piece of it with him, planted it in America, with ties to king and archbishop unbroken. Neither were the Puritans motivated by greed. They had no desire to raid, get rich, and go home (a desire, incidentally, that bedeviled Christopher Columbus among the "gentlemen" who wished to join him on his voyages, and that governed much early Spanish settlement).

It has even been claimed that the American Revolution was in fact effected by the Puritans, the Separatists. They broke the spiritual ties with the mother country, creating a separation of which the events of 1776 and afterward were a political and economic confirmation.

The Puritans' plan embodied a theocratic dynamic, verging on the demonic, that ensured the success of their settlement and generated influences and repercussions with an impact felt well past their own day.

> Consider that there are no persons in all the world unto whom God speaketh by His Providence as he doth to us.

> Have you not observed that there have been more awfull tremendous dispensations of divine Providence in New-England than in any place else?

> There never was a Generation that did so perfectly shake off the dust of Babylon . . . nor a place so like unto New Jerusalem as New England.

> How wonderfully suited is the going of Christ into America.

> If we look abroad over the face of the whole earth, where shall we see a place or people brought to such perfection?

> The *New English* Churches are a preface to the New Heavens.

Such were the stated beliefs of the Puritans.

Then, a significant change occurred. After the initial years of struggle, working a "remote, rocky, bushy, barren, wild-woody soil," the settlements began to be successful—Indians driven back, crops secure, the beginnings of a fishing industry, and the first stages of expansion. The intense spiritual rigors began to yield, to make accommodation for this new phenomenon of temporal success. There was a period of delicate, almost seamless transition, in which the Puritans' self-assurance, not to say arrogance, served them well:

> Look upon our townes & fields, look upon our habitations & shops and ships and behold our numerous posterity, and great encrease in the blessings of the Land & Sea. . . . Yes, there is not only a *spiritual glory,* visible onto to a spiritual eye, but also an *externall, and visible glory.*

> The gospel hath brought in its right hand Eternal Salvation. And in its left hand, Riches with Protection and Deliverance from Enemies.

> The Blessings both of the *upper and nether Springs,* the Blessings of Time and of Eternity.

> Such parents as have entered into a Covenant with the Lord may be assured, that the virtue, the blessing, the efficacy of the Covenant shall never be disannuled, but it shall go on to your children forever; by your Covenant, you have such a hold of God, that you may be assured, he will be a God, not to you only, but your seed shall stand before the Lord, to serve him for ever.

Thus, the *Arbella* and the *Mayflower* yielded to the Oriental trade and the whaling industry, and the "barren, wild-woody soil" yielded to Beacon Hill, Boston Brahmins, and Boston banks, with the sons of sons of sons blessed in perpetuity.

New England became an export item. Look at the place names across the country: in Ohio alone there are Plymouth and New Plymouth, Lexington and New Lexington, Springfield and New Springfield, Weston and New Weston; the principal city of Oregon is Portland, its capital Salem.

Still, for all the transition, the graceful acceptance of temporal glory, the old rigorous spirit—dour, perhaps injured—survived in New England as nowhere else. One is reminded of the encapsulated life of Emily Dickinson. Those other nineteenth-century figures— Thoreau, Hawthorne, Emerson—could be penetrating, perhaps soaring, certainly acute; but they would not invite descriptions as full-bodied, or full-blooded. Melville was an exception here, but it is well to remember that Melville was only half Yankee; on his mother's side he was Dutch and had, in fact, been raised in New York City and Albany.

Hawthorne was a major father figure for Melville, but the rush and enthusiasm of Melville's spirit overwhelmed the reserved Hawthorne. Later, Melville wrote that there was something lacking in the "plump sphericity" of Hawthorne.

Certainly there was never a more characteristic latter-day Puritan than John Brown: an awesome mix, well-nigh unbelievable in one man, of casual cruelty, intense and narrow passion, and the loftiest of ideals. The entire Abolitionist movement, in fact, was a New England project—a well-formed recrudescence of the Puritan ethic.

One of the clearest testaments to the power of the Puritan spirit is the evidence of what happened to some of its bearers as they departed westward out of New England: the flurry of strange sects, blossoming as the borders of New York, Ohio, and Indiana were crossed. Shakers, Mormons, Campbellites, Millerites. Ideal communities at Oneida, New York, and New Harmony, Indiana, the former offering free love, and perhaps incest. Having escaped the Calvinist umbrella, these people were like children suddenly let out of school.

*

One of the lovelier quotations in this book is from the diary of a revolutionary soldier—a farmer from Concord: "I like not these New York people, for they are craven and servile and filled with a lust for their property. Too much owning is a curse in a man's blood." New Englanders had a genuine hostility for people other than themselves; one is tempted to call it xenophobia. And this hostility seemed to focus particularly on New Yorkers. Hawthorne says somewhere that Melville could never seem to be at peace with himself; perhaps this was because Melville contained both hostile factions in his own blood.

Outsiders are often attracted to New England: they enter, submerge, and identify. But there is another kind of outsider who is attracted to New England, who comes to understand it as New Englanders themselves, or those who have entered, submerged, and identified, cannot. Such is Paul Strand, son of Jacob, native New Yorker through and through.

The lyric sense of nature, the stark theocratic purity, the practical sensibility, the unmatched craftsmanship, the careful affluence—all traceable to the establishment of the Kingdom of Heaven on Earth and its orderly transitions—all of these are clear in the photographs

116

that Strand, the matchless craftsman, brought back from his excursions to New England.

1980

24

Buster

I received a letter recently from someone who was commenting on a book we had both read, a recent biography of Buston Keaton by Tom Dardis. He complained that the book didn't really reveal the nature of the man, that Keaton remained for him still a beautiful puzzle.

I find this remark puzzling. For me, Keaton's nature emerges almost painfully clear: the physical abuse he took as a child, in the family vaudeville act, that immediately became a part of the way he was to survive; the suppression of emotions, the refusal ever to speak to anyone of his inmost feelings, feelings that found release only in the energetic enthusiasm for his work, in a succession of sexual conquests, and, perhaps most of all, in blasts of alcohol. But perhaps more revealing and most exciting in the book was the definition of what I would call his physicality. Uneducated, unburdened with any sort of literary language, his expression as writer, director and actor came entirely through his body. The extraordinary intelligence therein, the ideas that generated from it, were never separate from the sinew and muscle that put them into action.

Charles Olson said somewhere that he could not have a soul without a body. There is a dichotomy suggested here, which I find most intriguing, that may be demonstrated in many areas of the arts in America: the dichotomy between what we might call the intellectuals and the corporeals.

The intellectuals, generally, are borrowing and importing from Europe; the corporeals are developing something native to this country.

Keaton and Chaplin come first to mind. Both immensely skilled with their bodies, Chaplin—the European—is almost more a dancer, whereas Keaton is an athlete. Ballet vis-à-vis baseball. Chaplin's body is the embodiment of his ideas, it is pure and delicate; Keaton's body has the force of just that, a body—it is never less important than, or in service to, the ideas that are woven into it. In Keaton, thought and action are one.

One could argue—and I am tempted to argue—that this physicality, or corporeality, is peculiarly American, and those artists who demonstrate it and embody it are the deepest and most important people in their fields, for the simple reason that our history as a country, the physical nature of it, the discovery, exploration, settlement, building, etc., are so close to us, as opposed to the European experience, where even the modernization is imbued with inherited traditions.

Other pairs immediately suggest themselves in this dichotomy. Melville and Eliot, or Whitman and James. Williams and Pound— although Pound is a special case, his materials, so much of them, being imported, but his flavor, his speech rhythms, being physical and American. (Pound once told Williams that he, Williams, had never been west of the March Chunk switchback, but he, Pound, had known the pee-rar-ee.) We have Charles Ives, who poured new American cultural baggage into his work, and Schönberg—such an intellectual system! Harry Partch and John Cage: Partch couldn't stand Cage's music for the very reasons I'm talking about, and it is from Partch that I have borrowed the term *corporeality*. And, god knows, the best of American black jazz is marked by the hard, sometimes buffeting, physical impact of the notes.

There is a revealing vignette reported by Tom Dardis in the Keaton book. Chaplin hired Keaton to play a cameo role in *Limelight*. He offered Keaton a non-negotiable fee, below what Keaton deserved. Keaton didn't care, gladly accepted. Keaton performed brilliantly, endeared himself to the entire film crew. And Chaplin eventually cut a good portion of Keaton's scene, the implication being that he was a little annoyed with Keaton's success.

The tortured physical language in Hart Crane, the hard Maine rocks in a painting by Marsden Hartley, the incredible physical feats performed by Buster Keaton, never using a double . . . these are forces that come strong out of our own culture, with an impact on the whole corporeal being.

1981

119

25

Allen Ginsberg

The Visions of the Great Rememberer. By Allen Ginsberg;
with letters by Neal Cassady & drawings by Basil King.

It's no secret that Ginsberg and I come at the world from absolutely
opposite poles—a correspondence we had some time back, about
Melville, spells this out with some finality. If I wanted to be
superficial, I could allow myself to have nothing to do with him.

But I believe that his intelligence, his sensibility, are far superior to
everything else there is evident about him: his associates, his life-
style, his public image, his clowning, his religion, his sex, what I,
from my pole, would call the absence of formalism in his writing. He
works very hard at making himself out to be less than he is, an effort
at which he quite notably fails. He's a much finer man—much finer
looking, for example, when you meet him than his photographs would
indicate.

The kids all dig him, even the young ones just coming up: kids who
will read nothing else but Brautigan and Tolkien and sci-fi and
gothics will read Ginsberg, for what I take to be a combination of
right and wrong reasons. In a way, that sensibility and the energy in it
get to them, along with all the perverse goofiness, and I am sure they
are unable to separate the two.

They dig this ugly Buddhist thumbing his prick at the world, and
they dig his depressing, pessimistic, syrupy nostalgia so dear to their
own adolescence. But there is also the force of his intelligence, like
the second horse of a matched pair, pulling the Ginsberg chariot, and
this is a magnificent, energetic animal who captures my attention and
responses enthusiastically, and who does his share, I am sure, in
reaching the kids.

In *The Visions of the Great Rememberer*, he credits Kerouac,
himself and others with initiating, back in the late forties and early
fifties, various innovations and movements that later swept the
culture of young America. We all like to think that we're ahead of our

times, and in our old age, or even in our graves, we can lie back and watch the world reap the harvest we planted. But I question whether Ginsberg's strengths, his durability, lie in those areas of which he speaks. If that were all he had to offer, he would be merely the pop clown he is often made out to be—just as if we knew Ken Kesey only from the merry pranksters: Ginsberg a step earlier in that movement, but still, just that movement.

But Allen is a much older man than that, with much deeper roots. It may be a matter of years or a generation or two before his virtues separate out and become readily and unquestionably accessible.

Meanwhile, it is a pleasure always to read him, to be aware of those forces, often subterranean, never long neglected, occasionally surfacing magnificently.

In addition to the main text, the book contains a paper, a letter, really, addressed by Allen to Neal Cassady, and a series of letters from Neal to Allen. They serve, principally, to enforce the sense we already had, that Allen has involved himself, often deeply and painfully—almost to the point of appearing ridiculous, but never withholding himself for fear of just that—in the lives of people who fail to measure up to his own stature, who lack the qualities that manage to extricate themselves from his life. These people are the framework, Allen's frame. It is Allen himself, at the center, who matters.

Basil King's whimsical drawings go well with Allen's text. Whimsy is one of Allen's particular virtues, he leaps into it with special grace.

1976

26

Jaime de Angulo

The history of America is filled with accidental or deliberate crossings, confrontations, contacts-become-absorptions, where the white explorer-invader—Spanish, French, English, whatever—came in touch with the local native in such a way as to leave a positive mark—something other than death or wounding—on both. Such cultural crossbreedings occurred from the very beginnings of westward European expansion, across the waves of the Atlantic, the land waves of Appalachia, the plains and the Rockies, and the islanded waters of the Pacific—domain of Captain Cook, and the whalers—to the shores of Japan. From St. Brendan, perhaps, the adventurous Irish priest—to Admiral Perry.

It is the continental occurrences, though, with the durability that land and location provide, that most concern us.

John Smith made a beginning, in both New England and Virginia (in Massachusetts Bay, he cleared the way for the Pilgrims, and then referred to them contemptuously as "pigs of my owne sowe"). In the midcontinent, that indefatigable hiker and artist, George Catlin, painted and walked from Indians to Indians (not enough that he should cover North America, it is not so well known that he rambled the Andes as well). Innumerable well- or lesser-known anthropologists come to mind, such as Mooney, absorbing and absorbed by the Cherokees.

Certainly one of the most arresting of this group—and we follow the wave now, east to west, Appalachia to California—was that idiosyncratic poet-anthropologist, Jaime de Angulo. Lying drunk in a ditch with a shaman, he nevertheless retained a personal identity far more acute and dignified than a typical latter-day "visiting anthropologist" who skips in, gathers, and is out again, reporting to the educated community back home. (I'm told that the state of Alaska swarms now with pro-am anthropologists . . . the natives take to the hills whenever they see a white man zeroing in, armed with that six-shooter of the new frontier, the cassette recorder.)

One wonders for whom de Angulo was writing—whether in his journals of his own life with the Indians or in his re-creations of Indian mythology or in a novel of Hispano-Indian crosscurrents. Certainly he was not aiming for the popular market, nor for the academic world—nor was it an entirely private gesture, one doesn't have the closet sense of him at all. Insofar as he thought about an audience for himself, if in fact he ever did, it must have been something that intuition told him must exist, or could exist, or should exist, or, perhaps, will exist. As is so right and rare for the artist, this must have been a terminal and minimal consideration.

De Angulo established a quality of brotherhood with the Indians, brotherhood-without-loss-of-identity—a quality so important to Melville, which has led so many scholars and others to misread the Ishmael-Queequeg relationship in *Moby-Dick* as purely homosexual.

Son of a Spanish don, he purchased a ranch in northeastern California in 1913, and thus came into contact with the isolated and presumably primitive Pit River Indians. Trained as a psychiatrist, choosing instead to become a rancher, he was finally driven by his obsessive interest in these natives to become the most extraordinary anthropologist. Not enough to go and live with them, to share their torments and pleasures, to master the densities of their language, he effectively shattered within himself all artificial and natural barriers between white man and red, and *became* an Indian.

Such anthropology, as de Angulo practiced it, was, to say the least, unorthodox. "The University would not help me; took no interest; would not even give me enough money to have the records transcribed and made permanent on modern disks. Decent anthropologists don't associate with drunkards who go rolling in ditches with shamans."

So complete was his identification with his "subjects" that he was able to say, without condescension, "I followed that bunch for several weeks. I never saw such a goddam lot of improbable people." And one of the Indians greets him, after a separation: "Say, ain't you Buckaroo Doc? Well, I'll be darned! Where've you been? Remember that time you rode to the show and you didn't have no pants on, nothing but a mackinaw and your chaps and spurs, and you walked onto the stage with a bottle of whiskey by mistake, and for a while everybody thought you were one of the actors?"

But it wasn't all fun and games. Here he speaks of life inside their winter lodges, in the old days: ". . . you have to be an Indian to stand the crowding, the lack of privacy, the eternal squabbles of babies. And after a few months of occupancy the vermin was terrible. Once in a while someone would take out the old litter and bring in a fresh supply of pine boughs, but the fleas, lice, cockroaches soon returned."

With his extraordinary ear, de Angulo listened to the language: "I wandered around in the sagebrush. I was thinking about this Pit River language. I could see already that it was going to be a very difficult language to study, a very complex language, structurally complex. And yet the Pit River Indians were accounted one of the most primitive tribes among the California Indians, extremely primitive, just about at the level of the Stone Age in culture. And so I wondered . . . Could it be that there was no relation between language and culture? . . . By this time I had discovered that there were six modes in the Pit River verb: indicative, subjunctive, interrogative, volitional present or future, and optative (Oh, those so-simple languages of the primitive peoples!)."

Penetrating their territory in the early part of this century, de Angulo caught these Indians at a crucial turning: when the primitive mythology was still accessible, and yet the Indians had already moved, after their own fashion, into the modern age: "Indians had discovered a very good way to start the engine: prop up the hind end of the car with a jack, then start the engine by spinning the rear wheels, then kick off the jack, run after the car as it zig-zagged through the sagebrush, climb in at the back, and grab the steering wheel."

Not the least of his accomplishments is his re-creation of the wild and obscene wit of these primitives. Primitive obscenities have been recorded by many anthropologists but seldom presented with such force and delight. That which we moderns achieve with such strain and torment in such as, for example, Lenny Bruce, is an absolutely natural part of the storytelling, the myth-telling of these people, and de Angulo enjoys it with them.

What emerges in de Angulo—in his journals, his records of mythologies, his novels—is one of those rare historical moments of crosscultural affinity: the anthropologist-recorder-creator, if you wish—forges for himself—out of love, energy, the drive to understand—a role equal in lyrical dignity to that of the stories he is telling. It is the dream come to life—the dream of crosscultural and interracial brotherhood that Melville dreamt about, and brought into being, early in *Moby-Dick*, in the bridal bed of Ishmael and Queequeg.

1974

27

Whitman and Melville

Those two great giants, Whitman and Melville, bestriding the nineteenth century, provide striking parallels when considered together. And perhaps even more striking contrasts.

The coincidences in their lives are astonishing. Both were New Yorkers, Melville of the city and Whitman just outside, on Long Island. They were born the same year, 1819. Melville's heritage was aristocratic, and Whitman came from commoners; nevertheless, both men were of combined English-Dutch heritage—a mixture that seemed to produce more conflicts than one might expect. The English were a restless, adventurous people, settling and moving on, whereas the Dutch, at least in this country, were stable, rooted in the communities they established. I hope to point out that these varying degrees of restlessness—evidence, perhaps, of their mixed heritage— are keys to both men, providing both parallels and contrasts.

Another comparison involves their homosexual or bisexual drives. This is a well-known matter in Whitman's case—less clear cut, more open to speculation, in Melville. Nevertheless, Melville *did* write: "Nature, in no shallow surge / Against thee either sex may urge."

Another curious similarity that I don't think has been heavily investigated is the inability or unwillingness of either man to deal in any direct, human way with individual human beings. So many of the characters in Melville's novels are prototypes or archetypes— representatives of human or philosophic positions that he wished to establish. The English critic Ronald Mason has written: "Having limitless sympathy with man, he had dangerously imperfect sympathy with men and their activities; his preoccupations were with the elements, and the terrors and joys, the passions and speculations which close contact with those elements provoke." Similarly, Whitman wrote grandly of the "brotherhood" of man, but less well of individual, idiosyncratic human beings. (A sharp distinction should be pointed out here in passing: Melville's characters were the product

125

of his ideas—he was a philosopher; with Whitman, on the other hand, as John Jay Chapman has pointed out, "the revolt he represents is not an intellectual revolt. Ideas are not at the bottom of it. It is a revolt from drudgery. It is the revolt of laziness." This is not to demean Whitman, by comparison; laziness, in his hands, seems almost a positive energy.)

Nineteenth-century scholars have speculated at some length as to whether the two men ever met. Apparently, they did not—although we know they were aware of each other, late in the lives of both. It is hard to imagine what they would have made of each other at this stage . . . and it is not a surprise that neither left anything in writing about the other's work. There was, however, a critic, E. C. Stedman, who was personally acquainted with both men. He and his son Arthur visited them both, in Camden and New York. In a letter to Melville, the father mentions in passing, "as you said so much of Whitman. . . ." That's all we know.

Finally, in the catalogue of similarities, it can be said that the two men contrived to die within a year of each other: 1891 and '92.

*

Many of the distinctions between the two are obvious, while others are not at all clear. The discussion may be centered on the differences between the gentleman and the commoner, but the issue is confused by the changes that Melville went through during his life. Early, seafaring Melville was a Whitmanic rebel, identifying with the common sailors . . . the Pacific became his "Open Road." Whitman may have been the great celebrator of vagabondage, but Melville actually traveled—throughout the Pacific, to Europe, the Near East, the Midwest—infinitely more than Whitman. And one of Melville's Pittsfield friends reported that his neighbors thought him something of a "beachcomber." Thus, as D. H. Lawrence pointed out, Whitman and the early Melville had much in common: "The true democracy, where soul meets soul, in the open road. Democracy. American democracy where all journey down the open road. And where a soul is known at once in its going. Not by its clothes or appearance. Whitman did away with that. Not by its family name. Not even by its reputation. Whitman and Melville both discounted that."

But as Melville grew older, made a "white" marriage, bought property, became a father—and failed as a novelist—the gentleman, the aristocrat in him came more and more to the forefront. Whatever was going on inside him, much of his exterior behavior became conservative.

Curiously enough, Henry David Thoreau may claim, or have thrust upon him, at least a portion of the paternity of both Melville and Whitman. Whether from inner nature or force of circumstances, Melville gradually converted to the very sort of cautious Yankee that Thoreau was and remained all his life. Manifestly, a juxtaposition of Walden Pond with the Pacific Ocean is absurd. Or is it? We are all amazed, sometimes appalled, by the outrageous behavior of our children. Whitman's lineage, meanwhile, back to Thoreau, is well described by Wright Morris:

> The word *saunterer*, ill suited to Thoreau, slips onto the relaxed figure of Whitman like a glove.
>
> It is left to Whitman, the democrat en masse, to spell out what Thoreau glossed over, to yawp out over the roofs what a respectable Yankee would keep to himself.
>
> It is Whitman who carries to its conclusion Thoreau's admirable beginning. It is Whitman who *lives* the prevailing tendency.
>
> With his usual accuracy, Thoreau described his romance with Walden as an experiment—it is the safe Yankee testing the ice to see if it will bear the load. Whitman does not test or experiment. At the risk of exclusion, that is, he does not discriminate. All roads lie open, all friends are good friends, and all journeys perpetual. As Thoreau is the archetypal honest man, the square peg in the world's round holes, Whitman is the archetype that lurks even deeper—the professional tramp. The man whose business is no business, whose roof is the sky, whose house is the road, and whose law is the law of comrades.
>
> Thoreau might risk the *experiment* of friendship, but he would flee like the plague the *movement* of brothership.
>
> Having given sanction, if not birth to such a child, Thoreau would have been horrified to see it in operation.

*

Whitman at one point sheds his clothes and takes a sun bath: "So

127

hanging clothes on rail near by, keeping old broadbrim straw on head and easy shoes on feet, haven't I had a good time the last two hours!"

One could never imagine Melville—even in his beachcomber phase—writing such lines! In fact, Melville at no point in his life would have written something that he would call "Song of Myself." He knew full well that writing is an act of self-revelation; nevertheless, even if one is an exhibitionist, there are proprieties to be observed. His most famous first-person narrator, the Ishmael of *Moby-Dick*, is as elusive a character as one could imagine.

*

The gentleman-vis-à-vis-commoner issue has earlier roots in American history, much earlier than Melville and Whitman. Consider, first, the dispossessed, displaced soldier-farmers, paid off in worthless scrip after the Revolution, striking out in what became known as Shay's Rebellion. Earlier than this, there were troubles in Massachusetts with uprooted citizens following King Philip's War (1675). And, still earlier, there is Roger Williams and his difficulties with the authorities in Massachusetts Bay; and this is important because he *walked*, repeat *walked* from Massachusetts to Rhode Island—and this is the special, dignifying, characteristic activity of the rebel, the liberal, the beatnik, the hippie, the naturalist, conservationist and Indian lover: he *walks*. (Still earlier, there were Cabeza de Vaca and David Ingram.)

Perhaps Whitman never got beyond his Brooklyn ferries, but in *Leaves of Grass* he *strides*—or, as Wright Morris has it, he *saunters*. Strider or saunterer, he was the unconscious publicist, front man for a tradition already established: the tradition of John Chapman, Johnny Appleseed—more than Thoreau, perhaps, Whitman's authentic parent and original.

Son of a Massachusetts carpenter and farmer, Chapman emigrated west, wandered about Ohio for three decades, an "apple missionary," moving with the shifting frontier. His clothes were ragged and ill-fitting, his hair long and beard scraggly, he wore his mush pan on his head for a hat, and his feet were knobby, horny and frequently bare. The Indians discovered that he had healing powers, and they often sought him out. They also thought him crazy, and therefore regarded his life as sacred.

If Johnny Appleseed is Whitman's antecedent in this tradition, Vachel Lindsay is one of his clearest successors. Lindsay was much taken with Johnny, wrote about him frequently, and emulated him: he went on walking tours in the country, begging food and lodging, offering poems in exchange instead of apple seeds. Avoiding cities, he walked through villages and farms, from Illinois to Colorado, speaking of something he called "the Church of the Open Sky": "Thanks to the Good St. Francis who marks out my path for me, I start to-morrow morning to trot unharnessed once again." Others in this tradition would include the two Bartrams—and George Catlin.

Finally, closer to our own time, we come to the Beat Generation, the Kerouacs and Ginsbergs, and *their* descendents, the hippies: the scores of backpackers, hikers and hitchhikers of the sixties.

Opposed to all these are those whom we may call the conservatives or the gentlemen or the insiders—they stayed *inside*, wrote from what they carried within them, rather than risking the weather *outside*. Theirs was the sense of history and the cultural tradition, generally European—immaculate survivals of the Atlantic crossing. As already indicated, Melville is hard to pin down, depending on what stage of his life one deals with, but he certainly wound up an insider. Following in this tradition are Pound (a line of descent from Melville to Pound would please Pound not at all, but it can be found), and Pound's satellite, Eliot. Olson and Creeley probably belong here; they are perhaps bohemian but nonetheless conservative . . . the bohemian and the beatnik are different creatures, the former a transatlantic tradition, the latter Chapman-Whitman resurfacing.

American culture began as the transplanting of foreign seed in virgin soil. To the conservative, the emphasis is on the seed and its growth; to the beat, it is the soil itself that matters; the loss and flourishing of the altogether-altered seed becomes secondary, so that the soil, the land, ultimately outweighs the crop in value. Thus, it is through the liberal-beatnik that Nature comes in: our passion for land and conservation. The conservatives are concerned with man and culture, and find Nature, per se, uninteresting. Pound is not exactly a liberal-beatnik; nor is Olson what one would call a Nature poet.

The liberal-beatnik lets in *all*; there can be no exclusions. On the other hand, Eliot fled Missouri, and finally even New England wasn't cultured enough for him . . . Pound slammed the door on the Jew . . . as Olson on extra-New-England America . . . and Melville on all twentieth-century life (see *Clarel*).

But as surely as the door is slammed, some nut, daft in the head, skips out the window, pocket full of seed, and starts *walking* . . . the tradition surfaces anew.

*

One of the fascinating aspects of this Melville-Whitman dichotomy, conceived as a valid double tradition, is the fact that hardly any of the major figures fits neatly into either slot. Crossfertilizations abound. I have spoken of a line of descent from Melville to Pound, but there was also a good deal of Whitman in Pound. Olson and Ginsberg were good friends, had great respect for each other. And many a bearded backpacker is shrewd and knowledgeable behind that cloud of grass. It is often difficult to untangle the threads. But the capacity of a tradition to leave its own limits, to interweave itself intimately with its own opposite, is testimony, it seems to me, to its enduring validity.

1982

28

Herman and Hubert:
The Odd Couple

Elsewhere I have commented on what I take to be an artificial distinction between the nineteenth and twentieth centuries, pointing to the large debts—acknowledged in some cases, unacknowledged in others—that I feel Pound, Williams and Olson owe to their nineteenth-century forebears, Melville and Whitman. Without contradicting or abridging that viewpoint, I would nevertheless suggest that certain juxtapositions between the two centuries, if taken at a leap and with an eye for the absurd, can yield a kind of absurd significance, or significant absurdity.

What would happen, for example, were we to entertain together Walt Whitman and W. C. Fields? (Where would this happen? In a barroom? On the Open Road?)

How would Edgar Allan Poe respond, sobering up to Marie Dressler? Not exactly his Mrs. Clemm, his "Muddy."

Would Emily Dickinson and Errol Flynn even notice each other? (Are they the same species? Do they inhabit the same universe?)

Would Mae West get past the town limits of Concord on her visit to Emerson?

Would Thoreau have survived a year at Walden Pond had he opened his cabin door one morning to Stepin Fetchit?

These pairings are certainly absurd, and perhaps facetious—but not entirely so. And weighing the case with these Hollywood characters is certainly unfair to the match I propose to explore here: Herman Melville and Hubert Selby, Jr. An unlikely couple, certainly, but not altogether absurd; and Selby, I believe, will carry his end of the bargain.

My comments here have evolved from a chronological first reading of Selby's four published novels—*Last Exit to Brooklyn*, *The Room*, *The Demon*, and *Requiem for a Dream*. Some instinct has suggested that I approach him with Melville in the background.

131

*

If one wished to pick a watershed date, separating the early from the modern in America, 1865 would seem more appropriate than 1900. The culmination of the Civil War, with the assassination of Lincoln and the introduction of the era of the robber barons, altered the face, tone and volume of American life radically. And of America's best known nineteenth-century writers, Melville was the one most profoundly affected by these events—particularly if they are taken as a cataclysmic resolution of the racial issue. (It might be argued that Whitman's involvement in the Civil War was more direct, but Whitman never really faced the racial issue at the core of the matter: his Brotherhood of Man was in practice a Brotherhood of White Folks.) Melville was much more profoundly moved by these events than his awkward Civil War poems would indicate. And he understood the implications of the aftermath far better than any of his peers: the projection of late-nineteenth-century man into the twentieth, as these quotes from *Clarel* indicate:

> ... Sequel may ensue,
> Indeed, whose germs one now may view:
> Myriads playing pygmy parts —
> Debased into equality:
> In glut of all material arts
> A civic barbarism may be:
> Man disennobled—brutalized
> By popular science —
>
> Not only men, the *state* lives fast —
> Fast breeds the pregnant eggs and shells,
> The slumberous combustibles
> Sure to explode ...
>
> Asia shall stop her at the least,
> That old inertness of the East.

Late Melville was locked into his changing world, lamenting the loss of past values, but for the most part too bitterly prophetic to indulge in the luxury of nostalgia. A creature of earlier America, he truly experienced and survived the events of the watershed year of 1865 and inhabited uncomfortably the world that succeeded. (I recently heard of a man, a whaling captain, who commanded square-riggers on four-year voyages through the Pacific and then retired to

Brooklyn, to an apartment adjoining Ebbets Field, to spend his last years watching the Brooklyn Dodgers.)

I bring this up as background to a first reading of Selby, the first pages of *Last Exit to Brooklyn*. With this approach, one is struck at once by the different climate, the *thoroughly* twentieth-century climate, in which Selby is operating—a climate which he was among the first to recognize, explore and exploit. One way to identify this, to strike a comparison between Melville and Selby, would be on the "moral" issue, and here the key work of Melville's would be that tortured novel, *Pierre*. Selby at once seems to evince an amorality, a callousness to perversion and violence, that would have irritated and angered Melville but that Melville might have privately envied. *Pierre*, filled with hidden and hinted-at malevolent forces, is stabbing and stumbling in the direction of *Last Exit*, and it is almost as though Selby were retroactively exposing Melville for having worked himself into a lather over nothing.

In one way, a way quite different than Melville would have understood, Selby *is* a moral novelist: in the sense that catharsis, if allowed its own way, is always moral . . . a resolution of impacted forces. Of course, there is a simplicity to this idea that Melville quite rightly would have rejected, a simplicity expressed by Hemingway when he said that anything is moral that makes you feel good after you've done it. Melville would have taken Hemingway for a fool.

Still, this notion is not to be dismissed. In some ways, *Pierre*, by comparison with Selby, is dark and unclean. There is something oddly refreshing about Selby's extremes of sex and violence. As the TV soap commercials say, they "leave your skin tingling."

Pierre becomes involved with incest. By contrast, Selby's nymph, who calls herself Tralala—the whore who allows herself to be fucked to death—would, I imagine, be shocked by the notion of incest—she is much too *clean* for that.

Last Exit to Brooklyn is an extraordinary book, the most powerful, it seems to me, of the four. Story by story Selby is releasing his energies, releasing his horses, giving them their lead, barely holding enough rein on them to keep them on course . . . in a manner reminiscent of an earlier Melville, the one who wrote *Moby-Dick*. The long chapter "Strike" is one of the single most devastating pieces of modern American prose. Melville would have been appalled.

The final chapter, "Landsend," has peculiar connections with

Melville. As Carolyn Karcher has pointed out, Melville was obsessed with the idea of the Brotherhood of Man—from his life among the cannibals in *Typee*, to his crucial bridal-bed encounter with Queequeg at the beginning of *Moby-Dick*—not to mention *Benito Cereno*. "Landsend" is Selby's account of interracial life in the "projects," in modern America—and, again, Melville would have been appalled. Although surely he would have responded—"flashed," as they say now—to the chapter's characteristically Melvillian title.

*

The Room—although frequently powerful—seems to work less well as a whole. Here that acute and acutely characteristic twentieth-century affliction, paranoia, has entered and taken over. Selby indulges it fully. This was a luxury that Melville, sick as he may have become, was too fastidious, too steely willed, to indulge in—or it may simply have been unavailable to him in the social rigors of the nineteenth-century world in which he lived.

In any case, Selby seems to have lost some leverage. In *Last Exit*, there is a balance between author and material that gives the episodes of violence, cruelty and perversion that quality of unexpected, awesome exfoliation with which we are struck when such things actually happen: to be present as a kind of catatonic witness to the unfolding of a murder, a rape, a riot. In *The Room*, the reader has the first slight suspicion of being conned, the notion that what is happening is not really a *happening*, but the product of a conceived plan.

"He flowed deeper and deeper into himself, wrapped in the comforting strength"—this is *not* a line you would find in Melville—nor, for that fact, in *Last Exit*.

Last Exit may be taken as *process*, the exciting transition from the internal, frustrated dynamics of *Pierre;* and *The Room* is the final modern product of that process: paranoia, as a fait accompli.

Still and all, within that framework—and it may be that one simply makes an assumption of paranoia in dealing with Selby—there are moments, passages, in *The Room* of effulgence and clarity. He seems to achieve this effect by pursuing an event, a sequence, beyond those automatic and unnecessary limits that, as readers, we quite unconsciously impose on ourselves and our writers—so that we are shocked and delighted to find a greater serving than we deserve. In much the same way we are shocked and delighted by Melville, not in the turgid prose of *Pierre* but in the radiance of *Moby-Dick*.

Nevertheless, paranoia imposes its limits. *Last Exit* is the last chance to ride the nineteenth-century freeway before the twentieth takes over in *The Room*.

One additional note on *Pierre*. It is tempting, as I have shown, to plant Melville in the late nineteenth century and view him as a projectile aimed toward the modern world. Nevertheless, in *Pierre*—in which, at the very least, he foreshadowed Freudian psychology—he resolved the novel in a throwback to Greek and Shakespearean tragedy.

More pertinent to *The Room*, however, is a connection to another Melville story, "Bartleby the Scrivener." Selby's protagonist (whom, brilliantly, he has left unnamed) is a modern Bartleby. A jailbird, in solitary, he speaks of loneliness as his "friend":

... his legs hanging over the side of his bed and swinging back and forth slowly, rhythmically, his hands still clasped between his thighs. His head hanging from his neck. His friend tugged at the back of his throat and he swallowed automatically. His friend flowed caressingly through his body and closed his eyes with a wet ache. He felt his friend sing to him and he could taste him. At least he wasnt alone. He would always have his friend. He didnt have to seek him out. And he knew that his friend was right, that there was no point in trying any more. How many times had he tried? Endless and countless attempts, but the result was always the same and he always had to return to his friend and automatically swallow rapidly and repeatedly as his friend tugged at the back of his throat. Yes, his friend was right. . . .

They dont know what it is to feel the sorrow of the world. To feel the hollow, lumpy pain of hunger. Or loneliness. That terrible, overwhelming feeling of loneliness that makes you unaware of crowded streets and noisy rooms. That terrible loneliness that makes simple movements gigantic chores and weighs so heavy inside you that you cant answer a simple question with a yes or a no, or even shake your head. You cant even stare into inquisitive eyes. You can only feel the heavy loneliness flowing through your body and hanging wet and heavy on your eyes. . . .

Why bother? Why not just stand here with his forehead on his arm, propped against the wall. Whats the difference? Why go to all the trouble of going all the way from here to there? For what? Just to lie down under the covers? Why bother? Only have to get up again sooner or later. Why

135

not just stay here against the wall. Just freeze like this. Petrify. Turn into a fucking statue. Why not? Whats the difference? There. Here. Anywhere. Theres no difference.

Any or all of the above quotes might be taken as the *imagined* inner life of Bartleby, an inner life that Melville leaves absolutely locked and unexplored. Selby's "hero" is Bartleby all worked out, explicit, exposed, detailed—exploded.

In "Bartleby," the law offices looked out on an air shaft and blank walls—the air shaft resembling "a huge square cistern." In Selby's jail cell, our hero sits "on the edge of a bunk, or something, staring at a goddamn wall." He articulates a fantasy that might be Bartleby's silent interior—an inner life emerging like the pus of the book-length pimple that, squeezed and pressed as a motif throughout the work, finally bursts in the last pages.

"What miserable friendlessness and loneliness are here revealed!" says Melville of Bartleby.

Selby's despicable, solitary anti-hero nevertheless insinuates himself into the reader, gains unwanted ascendancy over him, just as Bartleby gained ascendancy over and eventually commanded his employer. But without exploding his pimple, without massively masturbating, as Selby's creature did, Bartleby finally dies in the fetal position the jailbird tried—and failed—to assume. Bartleby, in his unassailed interiorness, is complete. The jailbird, for all his pus and semen, lives on, without release.

*

The Demon is an uncomfortable book to read. Like all of Selby's characters, the protagonist, Harry White (very much a *white* man) is under the controlling cloud of what in nineteenth-century Christian terms would be called his *vice*—in this case, plain, old-fashioned lust. As a reader, from the very beginning, I feel that I am being powerfully seduced, i.e., set up—that all of charming Harry White's delightful frolics in the hay will lead to some sort of grim and horrible conclusion. In this case, Selby seems no longer directly paranoid but rather, like Melville, tormented by that very prosaic Christian notion that vice will be punished. It is curious, in the sequence of Selby's novels, to go from the violence, the paranoia, the sexual perversion of

136

the earlier work to this very simple moral posture.

Olson claimed that Melville got "all balled up with Christ"—and *The Demon* is a very Christian novel, the demon of the title being the lusts and the demands of the flesh.

For a while, it reads like a morality play: out of the welter of Vice emerges Love, Triumphant. But still we know that The Demon is not yet appeased.

And, reading on, we are confirmed: amid the Eden of Perfect Love, Marriage, Family, etc., the Demon—Promiscuous Lust (tits and asses, as Lenny Bruce used to say—T & A) reemerges.

Sure enough, our Hero—Hero Harry White—hits bottom:

> He went straight to Eighth Avenue, south of Times Square, and made the rounds of a few bars until he found a thirsty lush and bought a bottle and they went to her sour, roach-infested room. He could feel the sooty grayness crawl under his skin as he looked at the scummy walls and floor, and felt the gritty sheets as their foul stench reamed his nostrils.
>
> He fucked the sodden piss/sweat smelling mess next to him and then fucked her again before she drank herself to sleep.

One is reminded of Melville's Pierre when he leaves the idyllic Berkshires for Sin City, a sidewalk encounter:

> "I say, my pretty one! Dear! Dear! young man! Oh, love, you are in a vast hurry, ain't you? Can't you stop a bit, now, my dear: do—there's a sweet fellow."
>
> Pierre turned; and in the flashing, sinister, evil crosslights of a druggist's window, his eye caught the person of a wonderfully beautifully-featured girl; scarlet-cheeked, glaringly arrayed, and of a figure all natural grace but unnatural vivacity. Her whole form, however, was horribly lit by the green and yellow rays from the druggist's.
>
> "My God!" shuddered Pierre, hurrying forward, "the town's first welcome to youth!"

From the beginning, as I said, *The Demon* is an uncomfortable book to read, the reader having a sense of being set up. Nearing the end, one realizes that Selby himself seems to be experiencing little spontaneity; this is a *clinical* book . . . the author knows too much. There is little of that awkward stabbing that justifies *Pierre* or that makes Sherwood Anderson so attractive. It is the *clinical* that is the final result of the Freudian age to which Melville was stumbling.

Where characters and reader are being manipulated, as in this book, it is not surprising that Selby leads us into a melodramatic, show-biz climax full of flamboyant religiosity. I experience here, for the first time in Selby's writing, a suspicion of the purely commercial.

*

There is a gradual, marked deterioration, one book to the next, through Selby's four novels. In a way, the grandiose climax of *The Demon* is his swan song ... by the time we get to *Requiem for a Dream*, what we have is a competent, "shocking," commercial novel. Selby skillfully trading on Selby. All the driving fire of *Last Exit*—the author profoundly engaged in the flood of his material— has disappeared. Selby, in this last book, is not only fully in command; he is simply toying with his people. And with us. And here the Melville connection absolutely breaks down: Melville donned a customs officer uniform, submitted to a \$4-a-day routine, rather than assay this kind of literary commercialism.

The passion that pervades *Moby-Dick*, that in introverted form drives through *Pierre*, that similarly engenders the power of *Last Exit*, is simply drained out in what amounts to a "well-crafted" novel.

There is a danger signal in the early part of the book: the introduction of an artist. When writers start writing about writers, it's usually fatal, but even to write about an artist is an incestuous impulse, indicating a narrowing of range.

Oh, sure, the elements herein are properly "shocking"—in this case, drug addiction—and Selby's skills at character delineation are sharp and refined. But even the reader's discomfort that so characterized *The Demon* is fainter ... we know that disaster awaits the people we are reading about, but the author's hand is so distant, so controlled, that he has lost or sacrificed the capacity to unsettle us.

In the moments or passages that should be powerful or that appear to be powerful, I remind myself that I am not being moved. It is Selby trading on Selby.

Perhaps many would argue with my judgments here, considering this is one of Selby's best because it is so "well written." But it is just this flawlessness that I find uninteresting, as opposed to the driving, demonic energies of *Last Exit* and parts of *The Room* and *The*

Demon; energies similar to those that charged and bedeviled Melville's skills, as he barely maintained freeboard in *Moby-Dick*, and finally drove himself shapeless in *Pierre*.

*

Somewhere along the way, in the process of these four novels, Selby has lost me. Earlier, I found myself astonished at how easily, how naturally I went along with his people as they explored and experienced all manner of degradation. Now, in *Requiem*, the characters descend alone; I find myself mildly annoyed that I don't believe them and must follow them to the last page. (What happens to the old mother, Sara, is rank meretricious melodrama.)

In summation: I suppose Selby must be thought of as a Christian novelist. The Wages of Sin, etc. Strange, how the raw power of the earlier work and people captures our assurances, so that we suspend judgment, withhold conclusions, whereas in the later books the moral position gains ascendancy.

There is a simplicity about this from which Melville's lifelong uncertainty and ambiguities insulated him.

As I have proposed, Melville would have been appalled by Selby: angry, shocked—secretly admiring, perhaps envious. But Melville tossed and turned throughout his life in a state of philosophic irresolution. And it is just this "confusion," I suspect, that renders him so pregnant, that draws us back to try to deal with his irresolution for him, that makes him attractive to a reviewer as a possible "ancestor" to someone like Selby, or to the age in which Selby speaks. *Last Exit* offers the same kind of excitement, of density, of possible future openings, but from the other novels—where do we go?

1981

29

The Scene

Being a gathering and a ripping apart,
brimming with bile and bias, spleen and
prejudice, and offering, at the very end,
a glimmer of hope.

Perhaps the most striking aspect of Robert Hughes's recent book *The Shock of the New* is the assurance with which he treats the entire world of modern art—painting, sculpture and architecture—as a completed cycle, a fait accompli. One can imagine the dilemma of the contemporary painter faced with such a proposal: a world in which the economic values are inflated—art as investment—and its deeper values, the forces that drive him to palette and canvas, are adrift in shifting quicksand: one world finished, a new world not yet born.

The obvious question arises: does this proposal apply also to the world of poetry? Does the fragmentation of the art world—op, pop, surreal, hard-edge, postmodern, whatever—have its parallel in the fragmentation of the various schools of poetry? In a letter to me some time ago, a friend spoke of the "avant-garde primitivists," "the backpacking whale freaks," "the theosophists," "the I-must-be-hip-at-any-cost ideal personality clones of New York," "the new L A N G U A G E types," etc.

It would appear that the world of poetry is indeed filled with quicksand . . . and the poet thrashes about, searching for something substantial that will support his weight.

*

I shall at last see my complete face
Reflected not in the water but in the worn stone floor of my bridge
I shall keep to myself.
I shall not repeat others' comments about me.

140

This poem by John Ashbery represents at least one sad aspect of the contemporary poet's dilemma: Ashbery has chosen a kind of hermetic narcissism as a retreat from the noisy fragmentation of the modern world.

I would suggest that the majority of poets writing and publishing today have, at some early, elemental point, suffered a failure of courage. I would suggest that:

1. They are writing to defend themselves against reality rather than to engage it;

2. Many of them have forsaken the traditional artist's role of *making* and are satisfying themselves with simply *naming*; they have, in short, substituted nouns for verbs; and

3. Gertrude Stein, with the collaboration of the reductive and arrogant French, is the Great Earth Mother of this present American condition.

*

Your poet is often a frightened soul. And this fear seems to express itself as, first, self-indulgence, and second, a terrifying dedication to poetry. These poets have, in fact, placed the cart perfectly in advance of the horse: poetry trying to pull life.

This can be a very seductive stance: the poet, with his towering belief in poetry, would seem to have the True Cross. But, along with it—and this is evident in both his life and his poetry, damaging both equally—there is an ethical failure: we are dangerously close to the-end-justifies-the-means.

This is not necessarily Machiavellian, but the underlying premises are at least questionable: poetry is good, life is bad. The modern world is evil (oddly Calvinist, isn't it?); poetry is the only refuge. These assumptions are so easily made—it's almost like the click of a turnstile, you put a quarter in the slot and instantly you're on the other side. And a second world is created, a second view of the world you just left, which your poetry is supposed to celebrate and which will now be so difficult to recapture in that state of original innocence (you can never get that quarter back!). So now, irrevocably on the subway side of the platform, you do the only thing you can: churn out that daily poem, or daily six poems, or daily sixty, as your only

141

defense against the loss of Eden. (Yes, Eden . . . that evil, corrupt world that you willingly paid a quarter to escape . . . what is it when you can no longer go back to it?)

Such writing is a perfect adjunct to, perhaps product of, a drug culture. It is compulsive, obsessive—and addictive. The daily poem or poems as a demanded daily fix.

It is also the product of a culture hag-ridden by analysis and "therapy": the poet certifying his couch spoutings by funneling them through a typewriter and getting them printed.

Such poetry is not without public support—from patrons, foundations, arts councils, the National Endowment. (For over a year now this writer has served as literature panelist for the NEA . . . this is as good a place as any to confess my sins.) Insofar as both private and public giving to the arts are acts of cultural conscience, the donors are apt to seek out, or at least play along with, the trivial because the trivial will rock no *real* boats. To the typical rich, an overage adolescent sticking out his tongue at him is an image with which he is comfortable; it is *containable*. The rich—and arts boards—tend to recognize *style*—that is to say, no particular content or substance.

Compulsive poets, too, are perfect products of a consumer culture. They fit in, better than they can imagine, to that world they thought themselves to have rejected.

*

At some point in *The Shock of the New*, Robert Hughes speaks of the Surrealists, of how they abandoned the traditional artist's role of *making* things and resorted to simply *naming*. And Hannah Arendt has made the following remark (quoted by Jonathan Williams): "To quote is to name, and naming rather than speaking, the words rather than the sentence, brings truth to light."

Somewhere recently I have read comments about the cult of the writer in America, how the public is often more interested in the writer's personality than in the work produced. Following from this is the proposal that good writing is that which *radically differs* from the known or apparent personality of the writer—writing that, just because of this difference, "surprises" us. Conversely, bad writing is that which endlessly restates, without change or growth down through the years, the known and demonstrated personality of the writer. Such bad writing is called *self-expression:* the poet is *saying,* and often *naming*—but not *making.*

*

Clark Coolidge, Bernadette Mayer and the L A N G U A G E poets, have, in recent years, experienced some divergence, but I would suggest that they still have much in common. The L A N G U A G E poets, as one friend of mine described them, claim that "the poem should have no other reference than to other neighboring phrases, words & measures upon the very same page—a totally enclosed, hermetically sealed, self-sustaining world. . . . They stuck their tongue out at content, and closed the outside world, or even their own inside worlds, off from the center of their poems." As I shall propose later, there is a powerful connection here with Gertrude Stein, but more immediately, I think, the influences come from the abstract expressionist painters and from black jazz: the notion that the pigments on the surface of the canvas, the notes and tones that strike our ears, contain *all* that matters, the full range and substance of the work; that content or subject matter, in any traditional, referred sense, must be rigorously excluded.

In no way do I wish to include in this critical approach the painters and jazz composers themselves. It is an odd phenomenon that what works so magnificently for them, both in practice and rationale, becomes something altogether different when the medium, the pigment if you wish, is language. Tones of music and pure colors are able to penetrate our senses and consciousness altogether free of the burdens of history and meaning inherent in words. And the effort to expel from words precisely those burdens, all in the name of "freedom," comes across as an oddly Calvinist, Puritan gesture. It could happen only in a country that has tried to clamp upon itself the Eighteenth Amendment!

And this sort of piety produces, or will produce, not only its own demise but its own opposite. A recent book of Coolidge's—he is smart enough to stay ahead of his followers—is entitled *Own Face.* Out of the flat, anonymous plane of names and words, the ego is purified. The piety produces a sweet nostalgia for ego!

And in little of this, as I see it, is anyone doing what Melville referred to as "the ditcher's work" of making a book.

*

At a recent appearance in New York, I read a piece of prose—a section of a larger work—made up entirely of firsthand, subjective accounts written by schizophrenics. Toward the end, one of these unfortunates thinks of himself as Shakespeare reincarnate:

> Write, damnit—write something—write anything—write faster, faster!

> I write in columns on the wall, three feet wide, on huge sheets of wrapping paper, pasted together, running down the corridor, twelve feet an hour!

A poet in the audience, someone with long associations with New York, came up to me afterwards and said with a chuckle, "We'll make a New York poet out of you yet." It was a bit of banter, and I took it as such. But some time later I thought: these people, these schizophrenics, with whose words I was constructing my piece, were—yes—crazy.

*

After World War II there was a young GI who hung around Paris, attached himself to Gertrude Stein's salon, listened to The Great One holding forth. He noticed that if anyone had the temerity to interrupt her or even to present an idea at variance with her own, she would stop talking, stare at the offender, then start up again as though nothing had happened, but in a slightly louder voice.

He decided to test her. The two were out walking one day, Gertrude uttering her customary pronouncements. He interrupted. She stopped in her tracks, stared at him, then proceeded, her voice a little stronger. He interrupted again. Same process. Again. And again. Until finally Gertrude, standing on the street in Paris, was literally bellowing at him.

This self-confidence to the point of arrogance was her trademark.

And I suggest that it was not inconsistent with at least a part of the French national character. A comparison here between France and England is illuminating. Despite their bullying in Ireland, the English seem to know, to have accepted the fact that Britannia no longer rules the waves, that the sun *does* set on the British Empire. Something in the French psyche, however, that refuses to dislodge itself is arrested in the days of lingua franca, when Paris and France were the hub of the civilized and cultural universe. (American tourists with whom I have talked report without exception that the French are the rudest of all European peoples.)

Arrogant—and reductive. It was Francis Ponge who wrote a book called *The Voice of Things*. Things—and names. It is the French, I suspect, who are at the heart of this move to dismantle the paragraph, the sentence, to reduce language to individual words. Lacking energy or inclination to *make* something and assured within themselves that they remain at the heart of things, they have created and exported a culture shrunken and fragmented that shrinks and fragments whole segments of the American scene.

*

I would suggest that Europe is the land of nouns, America the land of verbs. The nearest concession to a verb a true European will make is at best intransitive, grudging. As in Samuel Beckett: "I can't go on. I go on." And Beckett, when asked why he wrote in French, replied, "Because French is the most beautiful language in which to say absolutely nothing." And Meridel LeSeuer, that grand octogenarian lady of the midwestern American Left—whose name but nothing else may be French—has recently said, "I'm doing away with the noun now. The noun is a capitalist invention."

*

"And it is no common coincidence if we can see our words shine in the dark, held like epitaphs frozen in their eternal order." These are the words of Edmond Jabès, celebrating The Word. And what a fine

145

introduction this would make to that mortuary that we call concrete poetry, where the words, the very letters, are frozen epitaphs, absolutely and forever drained of life and energy!

Roland Barthes: "This subject is never anything but a 'living contradiction'—a split subject, who simultaneously enjoys through the text the consistency of his selfhood and its collapse—its fall." Ah, that ego again, dancing on the flat plane of words!

Finally: "To go towards death, to make a death for himself as one would make a life. . . ." To Edmond Jabès, life and death might as well be equivalents.

*

Is it more than coincidence that so much of the "new" American poetry seems to flourish in the Bay Area, where the quality of the light is so Mediterranean, so like that light that drew so many of the French painters, late-nineteenth-early-twentieth century, south to the Côte d'Azur?

*

So what is the answer? For us? Here? Now?

One endeavors to shake off these "foreign devils," to rediscover and build upon those powerful native voices who have preceded us for two centuries. But to go back to the original question: Is the cycle of modernism for writers truly complete, as Robert Hughes suggests it is for artists? And if so, freeing ourselves of the reductive, what sort of ground remains?

In a recent letter, Don Byrd writes as follows: "What would you say to the notion that ART AS SUCH IS BY NOW A SENTIMENTAL HANGOVER OF THE TIME THAT THERE WAS A KULCHA, and that now the techniques of ART are useful as means of research, directing research, and presenting research, to make the necessary information available for public use? The thought is that the poem now is not usefully an object to contemplate, but as discovering the information and putting it into a context for use."

146

I wouldn't go quite that far. I think there is still energy to be infused in the poem, in the poem to be made, perhaps in a quite traditional way, building on Olson, Pound and Williams, drawing on Whitman and Melville, back through Shakespeare, all the way to Homer.

In other essays I have hammered on the idea of the physical, the physiological, the corporeal—the notion that the poem is not the product of the poet's intellect, of his "culture," of his sweet little heart or his tender little soul—but of his whole historical-cultural-genetic-inherited-physical presence, existence, and being.

Recently I was delighted to read an interview with Robert Creeley (published in a magazine called *O.ARS*). Creeley is recounting a trip he made through southern Mexico, where he stopped to visit a self-styled anthropologist named Franz Bloom:

> He said, "How would you like to meet a Mayan?" I said "Terrific!" He said, "Actually the man is a Lacandon Indian. He's the first person ever to come out of his particular situation *ever*. The first human being of that particular cluster ever to go beyond its stated boundaries and to move out of its area of habitation into this world."

The Indian comes into the room.

> What was extraordinary about this man was that all the senses were absolutely alert all over the body in the same way you'd experience the situation of a so-called wild animal as opposed to a domestic animal. I mean the sensory system was absolutely alert, not worried, but he was entirely *there*. I've never met a human being who was so completely where he was, not that he knew where he was or was determined to stay there, but was absolutely alive in the moment of each instant. I mean there was no abstraction in him. It was fantastic. I thought, "You *can* do it." I mean you *can* arrive at a consciousness that's present as opposed to one that's thinking about what happened last week or what is going to happen tomorrow as an imposition on the present instance. Extraordinarily fresh. He was healthy and, as one might expect, his whole sensory nervous system was absolutely incredible.
>
> In a somewhat like sense, as a younger man during the war and coming into contact with Gurkas, their central nervous system was fantastic. They again had not as purely, let's say, as this Indian but they had two aspects of that same centering of physical being without consciousness of being otherwise. So that when they were given things like sodium pentathol as an anaesthetic—the average Caucasian the average European or American will tend to go out certainly by ten in the count down. Most people are anaesthetized by the time they get to eight or nine. These men have been known to count to 100. I mean they have a central nervous

147

system that just won't quit. . . . I've seen . . . operations performed on these men when in all respects they should have been long gone with shock.

And again and again as I'm reading these various texts of poetry, say from Whitman's time to the, not to the present actually but to the '40s and '50s, the crisis seems to be endlessly the awful success of the process of objectivity and abstraction so that the mind seems to have almost no consciousness of the body it lives in even when it's preoccupied with that . . .

So there it is: the wild animal, with no abstraction, the centering of physical being, the sensory system absolutely alert . . . vis-à-vis the awful success of the process of objectivity, the mind with almost no consciousness of the body it lives in.

The noun may or may not be a capitalist invention, but it *is* an abstraction. In the verb, however, mind and body are integral, active, unself-conscious. And Creeley experiences that wonderful moment of illumination: "You *can* do it."

With this sort of possibility in prospect, what are we waiting for?

1983

30

John Gardner

The Sunlight Dialogues. By John Gardner.

In the spring of 1972 I was invited to participate in the Creative Arts Festival at Kent State University in Ohio. Consulting the road map, we found Kent to be 550 miles from our home here in the Berkshires, and being no longer nineteen, and I with a bad back, we decided to make it in two days with a motel stop along the way. The AAA tour guide pointed out the Treadway Inn, Batavia, New York, as a likely target, three-hundred miles the first day. I doubt if I'd ever heard of Batavia before, just a place with a motel.

This was our first jaunt westward via the New York Thruway, and I found it fascinating. (Recently, Ken Irby, with one of the most alert geographical minds, remarked to me about the boredom of this ride, but this must be the inevitable result of repetition.) Coming out of New England, as so many had before me, I perhaps placed myself in the role of a phase-two emigrant. In any case, the Massachusetts-New York border defined itself incisively both in the structure of the landscape and in the surviving architecture, and it is amazing how much of it, despite the savaging of both landscape and landmark, how much survives, to define character, a quality of adaptation and assertion. There is a New York State house, just across the border, on the right-hand side of the Berkshire extension of the thruway, a house well kept and clearly seen, by which I declare my entrance into the western state.

New York is grosser and grander than New England—the survival of large-scale farming, both poor and successful; the massive, solid, square village houses (there's a row of them, all together, somewhere along the way, Herkimer, I think)—conspicuous declaration of nineteenth-century prosperity that the Yankee might abjure (if a Yankee had money, he'd be afraid to let his neighbors know it).

Just out of Albany, we passed through the Albany pine barrens, which Don Byrd tells me are mentioned by Melville in *Moby-Dick*.

Then, joining the Mohawk River, climbing, ascending the natural river course through the valley, assured by it, we are unthreatened by the headlands that terminate just before reaching us. Evidences of the canal, the locks. The little industrial cities hugging the water power. Somewhere, before Utica, on a marsh bordering the river, a solitary great blue heron.

At Utica, the sense of a presence, almost ominous, to the north: the vast wilderness lands, both Adirondack Forest Preserve and privately held, that Edmund Wilson describes in his last exciting book, *Upstate*. We are only thirty-five miles from Talcottville, where he rooted on the edge of what is far and away the largest, privately held, unsettled and untraversed acreage in the state, a great white blob on the road map, with only the thin blue lines of small streams, feeders to the Mohawk.

The map shows that we pass close to the northern end of the Finger Lakes, but there is no sense of this area from the thruway. Rather the feeling of climbing toward and finally attaining an upland plateau, an area of grim calm—a wildlife refuge, scrub forests, windswept farms.

There is an old house, right next to the thruway, whose owner has nailed up a sign, facing the motorists: NO HELP HERE. GO BACK TO YOUR CAR, or some such. Retired samaritan.

Then, Exit 48. Batavia. (Also, a large sign, with an arrow: ATTICA.) And the sense, getting off the endless asphalt ribbon, after a full day's accretion of upstate sensations, a sense of final accumulation, a culmination.

Treadway Inn, of course, is something else. Square, smooth, modern, carpeted, Musaked. Master Charge will get you anything. It's Saturday night, and the racetrack crowd is swarming in the bar. (I found out later that it was at one of these motel bars, either this or perhaps the Holiday Inn, that the Attica guards celebrated drunkenly after the shoot-out at the prison.)

Somewhere, off there, in perhaps the real world, but certainly a different world, is Batavia.

The next morning, a search for the VW agency takes me through Batavia, and I get a little sense of the town, but not much—some of the solid, older houses, the trashed main street, etc.

Back, now, on the thruway, and somehow anticipating a repetition of yesterday's geomorphology, and instead, almost at once, an appalling arrival: big, dirty, amorphous, ugly, meaningless—or so it

150

seems from this vantage—the city of Buffalo.

*

When John Gardner's *The Sunlight Dialogues* was reviewed in the *New York Times*, the reviewer mentioned that the events took place in Batavia—and Gardner didn't fake it (as Thomas Wolfe's Asheville became Altamount), he named it: Batavia, New York. I ordered the book, and settled back for some reading: 673 long, large pages.

The book is often interesting, almost good, and finally a failure—all those 673 pages, for the working out of the mechanics of the novel.

What's good about it, beyond the naming of the town Batavia and the surrounding towns—Brockport, Warsaw, Akron—and Attica—is the settling in, the book, the people, the events, becoming a part of the area, emerging from it; not the literal history but a feeling for the kinds of people, two, three generations, uses and abuses of the land, attitudes toward the land, the inheritance of former adaptations to it, and attitudes toward that inheritance—and toward one another, the human responses. The presence—ominous, useful and meaningless, all at once—of the city of Buffalo.

The form of the novel, the decadence of the conventional novel form, the necessity of working out the mechanics of the themes, finally defeat the book. I came within three pages of the end before dinner the other night and felt no need to put off dinner, those three could wait until later, they couldn't possibly be important, by then.

On page 621, one of the characters says, "... we judge on the basis of the past. But tentatively, because there's always the future, p. 622." The flesh of the novel has been rubbed off, by now we have only the bare bones.

But again, what's good in the book: the sense of the place, decayed farming and families, hanging on or dispersed; Batavia the point of a triangle, the other points the prison at Attica—and that other sort of prison, the Tonawanda Indian Reservation. And just beyond, a dumb presence: Buffalo.

I find myself now with an impulse to pull up stakes here in the

151

Berkshires, move to Batavia, live there, become somehow involved, soak it up. It's doubtful that I'll do this, but the presence and force of the impulse indicate the extent to which I have been reached by the book.

Gardner, in his picture, looks to be young. Perhaps he was trying to write the Great American Novel before reaching thirty. His leading character, the Sunlight Man, holds forth at length, expounding a "philosophy" with which we are apparently supposed to be impressed. I found it a great bore.

Perhaps, some years hence, Mr. Gardner will go back, back to Batavia, and isolate it . . . the area, the towns, roads, routes, farms, woods . . . the people. Somebody should.

1975

31

Karl Young

Should Sun Forever Shine. By Karl Young.

There are three illustrations accompanying this book of poems: two are photographs of ancient mosaics, and the third appears to be a fragment of a mosaic, photographed severely out of focus. These graphics are unattributed, but the book was designed by the author, and they are a fortunate selection, cohering with the text in more ways than one.

I have never been much stirred by concrete poetry. The very premise involves a denial of what is to me the most essential element of literature: *movement*. How does one move, with feet stuck in concrete? This is not a joke, I mean this corporeal approach literally. Movement involves the body, and with the body of literature arrested in concrete, the head, released from corporeal responsibility, ascends, flying freely (sponsored, perhaps, by NASA!), into what appears to be absolutely brand-new discoveries and liberties. I use the word *ascends* intentionally because what is produced is a *high*.

So there we have it: the feet in concrete, the head in outer space. And the body of literature is denied possibility of movement. I am reminded here of a favorite word of Charles Olson, a dynamic of prime importance to him: *forwarding*.

Why, then, would I choose to review *Should Sun Forever Shine*—unless it were to dismiss Young with the rest of the concretists, playing their heady games?—and this is not my intention at all. True, the graphics described above—two in focus, the other heavily blurred—do suggest a kind of intellectual trick characteristic of the genre; and, true, the work is, indeed, concrete poetry. Ah, but with a difference!

(No doubt my lack of interest in concrete poetry has kept me ignorant of much of the work being done, and perhaps there are others making the kind of effort that Young is exploring here; but, if

153

so, I haven't found them.)

The difference is that within the strict visual disciplines and volatile possibilities that the mode imposes and allows, Young has introduced an historical dynamic, so that unlike the others, who seem obsessively titillated by the merely formal possibilities, Young's book contains a content, or substance, with a value at least equal to that of the form. So we have content and form, interfused and in balance.

I am reminded of a truism: "The content of a work of art matters only insofar as it be something about which the artist cares passionately." It is the caring for content that I find missing from most concrete poetry, and it is just this that distinguishes Young's work.

In a note, Young states that the poems are based on fragments of early Latin writing, some of it attributed to known writers, some found inscribed on bottles, boundary markers, etc. The sections of text vary in presentation—some plain and lucid, others extremely dense, to be read only painstakingly—blocks of words run together without spaces, or to be read vertically, or backwards. Making the effort to read this material—as the archaeologist "reads" the material he has unearthed—one re-creates the effort of probing and penetrating the density surrounding this gone historic epoch. And our satisfaction, for having entered into contract with Young, for having thrown our energy into the text as reader as he has as writer—our satisfaction is the sense of immersion in this ancient Latin period on its own terms, or on terms that Young has created that are in fact accurate to the material.

The strict and narrow form of concrete poetry becomes not an end in itself but a corridor through which we are led to this Latin experience.

I have been studying that blurred photograph again and have finally identified it. It is a fragment, part of the nose and one eye, of one of the clear mosaic faces. My effort has been rewarded.

1982

32

Richard Taylor, Stan Brakhage, Simon J. Ortiz

Girty, by Richard Taylor; *Film Biographies*, by Stan Brakhage; *A Good Journey*, by Simon J. Ortiz.

Having been published by Turtle Island Foundation myself (*Apalache*, 1976), I am perhaps suspect as a critic of other books on their list . . . the three here being considered were all produced by Turtle Island in 1977. But I beg the reader to read on; he will see that this is far from being an "in-house" review. The publisher (Bob Callahan) and I are good friends, but with areas of both agreement and disagreement—I think the following will make this evident.

It happens that I read these books in the order in which they are listed above, so that the experience became a sort of film sandwich: two superb, natural, whole-grain slices (no artificial preservatives), enclosing a filler with unlisted but traceable additives.

Girty is a marvelous book. The story of Simon Girty, renegade of the American revolutionary era—about whom derogatory jingles survived into my childhood—it is told in a complex of poetry and prose, document and invention, the elements scattered and interspersed, providing, finally, a wholeness, a *girtyness*, that it would be difficult for straight narrative to achieve.

I use the word "invention," and this is perhaps not quite accurate; nevertheless, Richard Taylor has taken a dangerous step, one on which many a historical writer has stumbled: he has created thoughts or stream of consciousness—what might have been journal entries had Girty been literate. To invent your subject's thinking and to juxtapose this with the known data of his life—this is risky; and for my money, Taylor has carried it off superbly. So well, that the slide from one to the other occurs effortlessly, and at times I don't even know or care which it is I'm reading.

The reasons for Taylor's success, I think, are twofold. The first may be embodied in an old truism: *the subject matter of a work of art*

155

matters only insofar as it is something about which the artist cares passionately. In Taylor's case, it was the passion, the intensity of his caring which led him into exhaustive research—so that by the time he sat down to write, he was soaked in *girtyness*—and his "inventions," as a result, come across as authentic.

There is no substitute for that passion, and for the effort, the hard work, that it allows.

Simon Girty was a curious and powerful force in the shaping of the white American mind. Kidnapped by Indians at age fifteen, he chose to remain among them, to acquire their ways, their wiliness in battle—or perhaps to fasten Indian patterns onto ways that were already natural to him. It was this—not only that he remained among the Indians, that he fought with the British and Indians against the Americans, but that he *chose* to do so—it was this that so infuriated his enemies, so violated every rational concept of which they were capable. His defection became a racial rather than a simple military matter.

Girty was perhaps as powerful as anyone in establishing racial passions as a prime element in the American character—an element not yet quite so virulent among the Puritans of New England, but that subsequently—after Girty—became part of our birthright, to be acquired by all immigrants, all ethnic groups, as they set foot on American shores: the passions that established the Jewish ghettos, kept the black in niggertown, treated the Indian as something to be exterminated, rendered the *niggerlover* the most hated of whites— and that flared most recently in South Boston.

One more note on this book: it is of just the length—148 pages— that it may be read in a single sitting. It is strongly recommended that it be read this way—the experience of Girty treated as an integer.

*

It is something of a jolt, to go from *Girty* to Brakhage's *Film Biographies*. Richard Taylor in *Girty* has somehow gotten inside his subject, and the book is the process of Taylor fighting his way out, the wrestling of author and subject providing the exhilaration. Stan Brakhage—who sketches for us the lives of Melies, Griffith, Dreyer,

Eisenstein, Chaplin, Laurel & Hardy, and others—gives the impression that he has joined (or perhaps established) an exclusive club to whose door only a few keys are issued, and his biographies are property to be enjoyed and understood only by the membership. He psychoanalyzes his subjects; he tells us the "meaning" of their lives and work; he talks down to us.

It is a curious thing about filmmakers and their approach to language. Prior to the industrial revolution, the artist's materials were relatively simple: writer and composer had pen and paper, the painter had brush and paints, and even where a contraption was involved—a harpsichord, say—the making and playing were never more than one remove from the human hand. With the development of photography, both still and moving, an increasingly complex machine involving all sorts of automatic actions interjected itself between artist and finished product; and, however much he may have wished otherwise, the machinery with its seductive fascinations diverted and often simply obsessed the artist's attention.

Filmmakers and photographers develop a jargon, a patois, that effectively keeps the rest of us outside. They are not elite by inborn nature but are rendered so by necessarily pursuing the labyrinths of their contraptions.

Turning to language, now, Brakhage seems to approach it as though it too were a contraption, filled with complex, moving mechanical parts. His is a hyped-up, jazzed-up style. Rather than being genuinely original, it is, I suppose, "avant-garde"—whatever in hell that term means. It is everything, in short, but natural.

Brakhage knows his subjects well, and his stories contain amusing and at times interesting bits of information. Such as: the first film ever shown on Vatican television was a Laurel & Hardy comedy. But where a straight narrative biography of a subject already exists—in the case of Keaton, for example—this will be a much more accessible and relaxing source for such information.

Thinking and writing, it seems to me, should be only as complicated as they have to be. Much less so, I would think, than a modern motion picture camera.

*

From internal evidence, Simon J. Ortiz, author of *A Good Journey*, is a contemporary Acoma Indian, with experiences both on and off the reservation. The book is a series of poems under five separate headings or categories. In a short preface, Ortiz quotes from an interview:

Who do you write for besides yourself?

For my children, for my wife, for my mother and my father and my grandparents and then reverse order that way so that I may have a good journey on my way back home.

. . . like some of the poems, that sounds simple—in the sense of "ah, the good simple Indian."

But it is not. And the reader had best read on.

There is a clue in the very first poem. He quotes a mythological figure, Old Coyote, and says of him:

Of course he was mainly bragging,
shooting his mouth.
The existential Man,
Dostoevsky Coyote.

A joke, yes. But the whole matter becomes more serious as the poems progress. Ortiz's accomplishment is to range back and forth across his genetic, racial, mythological and personal contemporary experience, from pre-Columbian Acoma to his most recent events in modern-day America, and he does this, first, in terms of himself and his own family, descendants and forebears, and then, by extension, all Acoma, all Indian.

It is strange, in a way, that this has not been done before, but, in my reading, at least, it has not.

In one of the poems, he tries to explain to the elder people that the state wants more of their land to widen a highway:

There is silence.
There is silence.
There is silence because you can't explain,
and you don't want to, and you know
when you use words like industry
and development and corporations
that it wouldn't do any good.

There is silence.
There is silence.

158

You don't like to think
that the fall into a bottomless despair
is too near and too easy and meaningless.
You don't want that silence to grow
deeper and deeper into you
because that growth inward stunts you,
and that is no way to continue,
and you want to continue.

One of the most moving poems in the collection is called "Burning River":

I will tell my son over and over again,
"Do not let the rivers burn."

. . . and he is referring to the time, recently, when the Cuyahoga River in northern Ohio became so saturated with flammable industrial pollutants that the river, literally, *caught on fire.*

Simon J. Ortiz, contemporary Acoma Indian, telling his own child, he who will survive him, who will inherit what there is in America to inherit, "Do not let the rivers burn" . . . the full weight of his inheritance comes to bear here, impinging painfully on the good journey that he so wishes for his son, his descendant.

As in *Girty*, there is a wholeness in this book that only becomes apparent when one reads it through.

N.d.

33

Stampers and Hawkers

On August 1st this past summer—Herman Melville's birthday—the U. S. Postal Service held ceremonies in New Bedford in connection with the first-day issue of a new Melville stamp, part of the literary arts series. As one of Melville's surviving descendants—I am a great-grandson—I was invited to attend, representing the family.

My wife and I drove down the day before. It was a typical sweltering summer day. We checked into the Whaler Inn, kindness of the New Bedford Post Office, and made tracks as fast as we could for Horseneck Beach and a swim in one of the two great oceans on which Melville had voyaged.

The next day blossomed even hotter: a soggy, blistering day, and even at the harbor there was not a breath of wind. We made our way to the Whaling Museum, where, an hour before the stamps were to go on sale, the collectors were already lining up. We were escorted to the director's office where we drank coffee and hobnobbed with some of the visiting dignitaries. These included the assistant postmaster general from Washington; the postmaster of New Bedford; the mayor of New Bedford; a rear admiral from the Coast Guard; the president of the Melville Society; a chaplain; the port director of customs; assorted other local postmasters; etc. Among such I was a sort of minister without portfolio, with nothing but my bloodline to offer—and feeling a little bit silly about it.

At the appointed hour, we were lined up military fashion and marched through what had now become a seething mob of stamp collectors, to the auditorium, where we took our chairs on the platform. Gracing the ceremonies were the First Marine Band and Ceremonial Guard, in full button-down regalia—on this steamy, steamy hot day! Following opening remarks, we had the presentation of colors, the National Anthem and the invocation. We were patriotic and blessed, and ready to sail into a sea of speeches—which indeed followed. (During one of these, Dr. Milton Stern, president of the Melville Society, scribbled a note on an envelope and slipped it to me: "What do you think Melville would have made of all this?" I wrote back, putting it in quotes: "I don't believe it!")

To vary the program, we had a group of musical selections: a rousing performance of "Stars and Stripes Forever," and some semiclassical pieces, with that peculiar tone that occurs when a good military band tries to be "aesthetic."

With the conclusion of the final speech, and the presentation of albums, we filed out of the auditorium, and I thought, that's that.

But that was not that. That was just the beginning. There occurred now a phenomenon that left me shaken, and that still somewhat mystifies me. There were more than four hundred in the auditorium, most of them stamp collectors, and, picking me out from among the other dignitaries, a swarm of them descended on me, seemingly all at once, all shoving programs and ballpoints under my nose, demanding my autograph. I'm as vain as the next man, and anyone who asks for my autograph generally has my attention. But this turned into a mob scene, I scribbled and scribbled and scribbled, the sweat of my brow fogging my glasses, and I began to think to myself: Who are these people? What do they think they're getting? I'm three generations removed from The Great Man, and yet they seem to think they're getting a piece of Him, as though I were Herman himself signing their programs. One insistent woman demanded that I sign *six*—"for the grandchildren." After nearly an hour of this, when my fingers were cramping and my legs felt rubbery, the last of these strange souls finally departed.

We were collected once more and made our way over sunbaked sidewalks to the harborside. Here we boarded the U.S. Coast Guard cutter *Unimak* and sat down at tables on the afterdeck. Without benefit of canopy or awning, we lunched on elegant broiled haddock under the broiling, broiling sun—and listened to more speeches. My wife thought she was going to faint.

When it was finally over, the crew stood at attention and piped us ashore.

We drove back to the Whaler Inn, slithered out of our sopping clothes and into bathing suits, and headed once more for Horseneck and a cleansing, cooling plunge into the waves. Swimming under water and on the surface, bobbing with the waves, bodysurfing, I thought again of that swarm of locusts that had descended on me. I thought of Dr. Stern's question: "What do you think Melville would have made of all this?" I recalled that *Moby-Dick* had been published in 1851, when Melville was thirty-two; that it was panned by the critics and sold poorly; that Melville lived and wrote for another forty years after this, and died in almost complete obscurity; and that still another thirty years passed before interest in *Moby-Dick* began to develop. I thought: suppose it had been Melville himself, and not I, who had signed all those programs? What, indeed, would he have made of it?

Finishing our swim, we went back to the Whaler Inn for a dinner of motel fish and an evening watching the Red Sox lose another one on television.

There are some things in this world that are just too mad to contemplate.

*

I have no idea whose birthday falls on September 16th. But that day, here in the Berkshires, blossomed sparkling clear. Following a day and night of humidity and rain, a weather front passed through, and the morning air was fresh and crisp, with a northwest breeze. I had become interested in the migration pattern of hawks and discovered to my surprise that we were only a forty-five-minute drive from two of the better spots in the northeast from which to observe these flights.

We had gone first to Mt. Tom—or, more properly, Goat Peak, adjacent to Tom. Here there is a steel tower rising above the treetops, and the platform at the top offers a panoramic view: the Connecticut River valley, with the oxbow; Mt. Monadnock; the tall buildings of the University of Massachusetts; Westover; Northampton, Easthampton, Holyoke, Springfield and Hartford. It had been a beautiful sunny day, but the hawk flights were disappointing: only a few birds, and these at a distance. The greatest excitement came from an eagle—whether immature bald or golden could not be determined. (My fellow observers, all strangers to me, were obviously experts, with years of study and watching behind them.)

This day—September 16—we decided to go to another spot, also nearby. It is simply a hilltop, located in—ah, no, dear readers: I think I shall keep this to myself. It is one of the most spectacularly beautiful and apparently little-known spots here in the Berkshires, and if I locate it and publicize it, you and your family and friends will discover it and flock to it, and it will cease to be what it is now: the top of the world, in a near-perfect state of nature.

It is just a bare hilltop, and not particularly high, an easy climb from the road. It is spectacular, though, because the land around it is all slightly lower, and one looks for miles and miles and miles in any direction before discovering a higher configuration, so that the sky is an enormous blue bowl, and one stands on the hilltop at the center of what seems a near-perfect circle. Well-known mountains were visible, some at a great distance, but I shall not name them, dear readers, for there lurks among you someone with a cartographic mind who would use this information to help pinpoint our hilltop.

There were two hawk-watchers present when we arrived, and perhaps eight or ten others showed up as the morning wore on. They were all carrying picnic lunches, folding chairs, and the inevitable binoculars; they were there for the day, to make an official count for their local chapter of the Audubon Society.

On the platform at Mt. Tom, and here on this hilltop, I became aware at once of a rare kind of camaraderie. It was rare in that it mixed openness and friendliness with respect for one's privacy. In both places, we were outsiders: amateurs among experts. I quickly discovered that if I wanted to be alone with my thoughts, or with the birds, or with nature, they would leave me alone; but if I wanted to ask questions or share perceptions, they were more than helpful, going out of their way to indoctrinate us into the wonderful world of hawks, without being patronizing or condescending.

At Mt. Tom I had been wearing my Red Sox cap, and this brought me into conversation with some of the men, mostly older, all of whom were dedicated baseball fans, as well as bird-watchers. I thought of John Kieran, the late sportswriter for the *New York Times*, who was also a serious bird-watcher and naturalist. I have meditated some on this affinity, between bird-watching and baseball.

Here on the hilltop, we had come only for the morning, had not brought lunch. Our new friends opened their picnic boxes, offered to share with us. We politely declined.

At both places, I observed and tried to speculate on the back-grounds of these people. They seemed to come from different walks of life, some giving evidence of the "advantages," others clearly from the working class. They were brought together by their single compelling interest.

I felt, too, that their response to the world of birds was an aesthetic experience; but, in most cases, it was the single aesthetic in their lives. These were not gallerygoers, poetry readers, music lovers, but their artistic passion was every bit as powerful. One of my favorites among them was a young man in ragged jeans, a work shirt, a baseball cap on backwards, and his hair in a pony tail. He described what is called a "kettle" of hawks rising in a thermal wind, reaching the top, and then, one by one, peeling off: "That's neat," he said. "Neat." That single monosyllable said it all.

When we first arrived, the sky was clear, with only a few clouds on the horizon. Although the sun was warm, it was breezy and cool enough for a down jacket. Initially, the hawks were few and distant. We stood or sat among the low-bush blueberries, conversed casually, and scanned the horizon. The first excitement was a flight of twelve broadwings, directly overhead. By now some wispy cumulous clouds had spread over us, and we lay on our backs looking directly up at the seemingly chaotic, swiftly moving patterns of flight, in and out among the blue of the sky, and the white and soft gray of the clouds. The birds were near enough to be seen with the naked eye, but to be seen much better of course through the glasses. The whole flight lasted only a few moments, and they were gone.

Later there was a much larger kettle, again directly overhead. As before, we lay on our backs, the glasses lifted and lowered, lifted and lowered. This flight lasted for several minutes, and the official count came to 214. If you think that's a lot, dear readers, consider: on 13 September 1983, at Mt. Wachusett, during the space of one hour— 12 noon to 1 P.M.—the official count of broadwinged hawks came to 16,216! No such prodigious numbers at our hilltop. Still, the few minutes that it took those 214 to pass were strangely exciting.

At Mt. Tom we had been disappointed because the birds were few, and distant. Here, the birds were more plentiful, but similarly distant; and it occurred to me that that's part of the aesthetic, the excitement: those magnificent creatures, swirling, soaring, rising, diving— keeping their distance. Closer, they would lose their wildness, which was their signal virtue.

*

A little after midday we took our leave. On the way home my wife pointed out to me how strange was the contrast between these two events of our summer: New Bedford and the hawk-watch.

Strange, indeed.

First, the weather, that framework in which all events occur, and which is seldom far from the attention of a New Englander: there was the cloying, steamy humidity of New Bedford . . . and the brisk, dry, early-fall warmth-and-chill on the hilltop.

I thought of Herman Melville, the man whom we were presumably celebrating in New Bedford, the man whose restless, roaming spirit carried him to the South Seas . . . as the instinct of the broadwings overhead led them in their southward migration.

I thought of the people: the stampers and the hawkers. The stampers, cornering me, crowding me, clutching their programs and ballpoints in their sweaty palms, seemed a people possessed, as though fighting an unseen enemy, seeking security in their collections and autographs. The hawkers, on the other hand, were without an ax to grind.

There was the almost military formality of the ceremonies in New Bedford, vis-à-vis the relaxed informality, both at Mt. Tom and the hilltop.

For the stampers, there seemed some demonic significance in possessing a family member's autograph. I wondered: suppose I were to tell the hawkers who my great-grandfather was? I imagine they would be polite about it, but I doubt that they would really care. I would neither rise nor fall in their estimation. And the hawks themselves wouldn't give a tinker's damn!

These thoughts give me great pleasure.

1984

The author has lettered and signed 26 copies
of this edition.